Quirky Tails

D1040494

MORE ODDBALL STORIES

Quirky Tails

Quirky? You can say that again.

Look at it. It's so small there is only just enough room to poke in one pea at a time. He can't talk, he can't stick out his tongue and he can't eat.

You'll be speechless.

A face on your tonsils.
A headless chicken.
Life with an undertaker.
A living copy – of yourself.

More quirky stories from the quirky mind of Paul Jennings.

Books by Paul Jennings

Unreal!
Uncanny!
Quirky Tails
Unbelievable!
Unbearable!
Unmentionable!
Undone!

PAUL JENNINGS

Quirky Tails

MORE ODDBALL STORIES

Puffin Books

PUFFIN BOOKS
Published by the Penguin Group
Penguin Books USA Inc., 375 Hudson Street, New York, New York 10014, U.S.A.
Penguin Books Ltd, 27 Wrights Lane, London W8 5TZ, England
Penguin Books Australia Ltd, Ringwood, Victoria, Australia
Penguin Books Canada Ltd, 10 Alcorn Avenue, Toronto, Ontario, Canada M4V 3B2
Penguin Books (N.Z.) Ltd, 182–190 Wairau Road, Auckland 10, New Zealand

Penguin Books Ltd, Registered Offices: Harmondsworth, Middlesex, England

First published in Australia by Penguin Books Australia Ltd, 1987
First published in the United States of America by Puffin Books,
a division of Penguin Books USA Inc., 1990
This edition first published by Penguin Books Australia Ltd, 1994
Published in Puffin Books, 1995

1 3 5 7 9 10 8 6 4 2

Copyright © Paul Jennings, 1987

All rights reserved

ISBN 0-14-037637-2

Printed in Australia by Australian Print Group
Set in Baskerville

The words from the Australian ballad, 'The Wild Colonial Boy' which appear on pages 57 and
58 are reproduced from the *Penguin Australian Song Book* compiled by J.S. Manifold and first
published in 1964.

For Tracy

CONTENTS

SNEEZE 'N COFFIN

The reporter looked at Tracy with a smile. 'I'd like to talk to you about your job,' he said. 'It would make a good story for the paper. Not many teenagers go into this line of work. Just how did you get started in it in the first place?'

'Well,' answered Tracy. 'It all began when Mum told me she was going to remarry.'

'I'm sorry,' said Mum. 'But I'm getting married whether you like it or not.'

'But Mum,' I started off.

'No buts,' she cut in. 'I'm lonely at night when you and Andy have gone to bed. And anyway, I love Ralph. He is a lovely man. I thought you liked him too.'

'I do,' I said. 'It's not him I don't like. It's his job. He buries people in the cemetery.'

'What's that got to do with it?' she asked hotly. 'I'm not going to stop loving Ralph just because he is an undertaker. You don't judge a person by their job.'

'It's embarrassing,' I said. 'Last night he took us down the street to the fish and chip shop in his funeral wagon.

1

Do you realise that our tea was brought home in a hearse? The same car that is used to cart dead bodies around. All the kids were laughing. One idiot laid down on the footpath with a flower in his mouth as we went by and pretended he was dead. Old Mr Manor takes his hat off as we go past. It's the absolute pits going around in a hearse. Why doesn't he get a normal car like other people?'

'Ralph can't afford another car at the moment,' said Mum sadly. 'Business has been bad lately.'

'I suppose he is waiting for an axe maniac to move into town or perhaps things would pick up if we introduced the bubonic plague.'

'That's not funny, Tracy,' Mum yelled. She was starting to get angry so I decided to give in.

Anyway, I had to agree with her. Ralph was a nice bloke. It was just bad luck that he made his living by burying dead people. And animals. That's something else I should mention. He had a pet cemetery as well. He used to collect dead pets and bury them in a little plot just outside of town.

Well, Mum and Ralph got married and my little brother Andy and I had a new stepfather. We all went off to the snowfields together on our honeymoon. In the hearse of course. I tried everything I could think of to talk Ralph out of taking the hearse but it was no use. 'It's just right for the snow,' he said. 'We can put the skis in the back and there's plenty of room for the luggage.'

It was terrible. A real shame job. Every day we arrived at the bottom of the ski slopes in the grey hearse with:

2

written on the door. People came rushing over to see who had been killed.

At lunch time we would get out our portable barbecue and set it up behind the wagon. Ralph would cook chops and steak. A man came over and said that he knew that beef was expensive at the moment but wasn't this going a bit far? We were the laughing stock of the ski slopes. People called us 'The Skiing Cannibals'.

I was sure glad when that honeymoon was over. It was a nightmare. Not that things improved when we got home. They didn't. Ralph moved in with us and straight away built a workshop at the bottom of the yard. 'What's it for?' I asked. 'And why hasn't it got any windows?'

He looked around furtively. 'Don't tell Andy,' he said. 'Your little brother is too young to understand. It's a workshop for making coffins.'

'What?' I screamed. 'What will my girlfriends think if they know we have coffins at the bottom of the garden?'

'Don't tell them,' said Ralph. 'What they don't know won't hurt them.'

'But *I* know,' I retorted. 'I'll never get to sleep knowing there are coffins in our home.'

'Don't be so sensitive,' said Ralph. 'They are just empty coffins. I wouldn't bring the corpses back here. They stay at the funeral parlour until the burial. You should try to get used to it. One day I am going to take you in as a partner in the business.'

'Over my dead body,' I said.

3

Ralph didn't even crack a smile. He had his heart set on me joining the business. He looked so upset that I even felt a bit sorry for him.

Just then Andy came into the room. 'What are those things that you are making?' he asked pointing at three half-finished coffins.

Ralph didn't bat an eyelid. 'Boats,' he lied. 'I am making some boats.'

Andy was only seven and he believed it. 'Wow,' he said. 'Fantastic.'

It was a stupid thing to say and I knew it would cause trouble. I wasn't wrong. Two days later, when I was at home on my own, the phone rang. It was the Portland Police. They asked me to come down to the main beach at once.

When I got there I saw the most humiliating thing of my life. The beach was lined with hundreds of people – all of them shrieking with laughter. Some of them were rolling around on the sand holding their sides. They were all laughing at the same thing. My brother Andy. He was paddling a coffin around in the water among the swimmers.

He had loaded a coffin up on my surfboard trailer and pulled it down to the beach behind his bike. Then he had launched it out onto the water. He really thought it was a boat. I couldn't believe it.

Of course the whole thing was in the paper and on the TV. The whole family was disgraced. Everyone knew that my little brother had been sailing around in a coffin. I couldn't look the girls at school in the eyes for months. And Ralph didn't even care. 'It was a good coffin,' was all he said. 'It didn't even leak one drop.'

4

After that things just went from bad to worse. Mum decided that I would have to help Ralph on weekends as he couldn't afford to pay his helper overtime. 'I'm not going near corpses,' I said. 'No way.'

Ralph looked hurt. He really hoped that I would become an undertaker like him. 'That's all right,' he said. 'You can help with the pet side of the business. I don't expect you to go to the funerals of people just yet.'

This didn't sound too bad but in fact it turned out to be another disaster. Ralph used to pick up people's dead pets in the hearse and take them out to the pet cemetery. It was amazing what some people would do. There were little graves for dogs, cats, canaries, mice and rabbits. There were big graves too. You name it and it was buried there.

A lot of people think that their pets are human. You take old Mrs Trapp, for example. She wanted a special funeral for her cat Fibble. 'Come round at four o'clock and fetch him,' she said on the phone. 'I want a proper burial with a priest, a hearse and flowers. Nothing is too good for my poor Fibble,' I could hear her sniffing on the other end of the phone. I shook my head. I just couldn't understand it. Fancy paying money to have a funeral for a cat.

'Good,' said Ralph. 'Four o'clock will be fine. I have to do a pick-up at the zoo at three. We can call at Mrs Trapp's house for Fibble on the way back.'

I groaned. 'What died at the zoo? I hope it wasn't the elephant.'

'No,' said Ralph. 'It's a baby giraffe.'

When we reached the zoo, Mr Proud, the director, was standing next to this poor dead giraffe. He was upset. 'I

5

want you to do a good job,' he said. 'Dig a nice deep hole. I want this giraffe to rest in peace. Be careful with him. His last journey should be slow, dignified and gentle. I am going to drive to the pet cemetery and make sure you do it properly.'

His eyes were red and swollen. I could see he loved this giraffe a lot. He drove off to the cemetery and left us to load up the giraffe.

It was only a baby one but it was heavy. And it was too big for the trailer. Its long neck and head hung over the back and touched the ground.

'We can't have that,' said Ralph. He tied a rope around its little horns and pulled. The giraffe's head lifted up off the ground. 'There's no way to tie it up and stop the head from drooping,' Ralph told me. 'You will have to stand in the trailer on top of the giraffe and pull on the rope to keep its head up in the air.'

'You're joking,' I exclaimed.

'No,' said Ralph. 'It's the only way. 'I'll drive slowly so you don't fall off.' Without another word he climbed into the hearse and started to drive away. I only just had time to scramble onto the dead giraffe and pull its head up.

We went out of the zoo and along the street. Did Ralph go around the back way so that no one would see us? No he did not. He went straight through the middle of the town. You can imagine what we looked like. A hearse, followed by a trailer with a dead giraffe on it. And on top of the giraffe, a girl hanging onto a rope trying to keep its head from dropping onto the road.

It brought the traffic to a standstill. Everyone yelled and shouted. People rushed out of the shops to see the sight. It was worse than Andy and his coffin boat. We

6

stopped at every traffic light, exposed for all to see. I have never been more ashamed in my life. But there was worse to come.

My arms started to get tired. A giraffe's neck is heavy. The head drooped closer and closer to the road until at last it started to rub on the bitumen. I heaved it up but I couldn't hold it for long. 'Stop,' I screamed to Ralph. 'Stop. Its head is rubbing on the ground.' Ralph kept going. He was listening to the grand final on the radio and couldn't hear me. So we kept on in the same way all the way to the pet cemetery. The poor giraffe's head must have banged on the road a hundred times.

When we finally arrived, Mr Proud was waiting for us and dabbing at his red eyes with a handkerchief. He walked over to his dead giraffe to inspect it. Suddenly he stopped. His eyes nearly popped out of his head. 'What's this?' he screamed. 'My poor giraffe. Where is its nose? Its nose is gone. What have you done with its nose?'

'Sorry,' I said. 'It got rubbed off on the road. Its head was too heavy for me.'

'You stupid girl,' he yelled. 'You fiend.' He came towards me with his hands held out like claws. He had murder in his eyes.

I turned and ran. I fled down the road with the enraged Mr Proud behind me. He chased me for miles but in the end he gave up and went back.

I walked home with tears streaming down my face. I was sick to death of Ralph and his funerals – animal and human. My life was turning into a complete mess. I made up my mind never to have anything to do with Budget Funerals. There was no way I would ever get involved again. And as for becoming a partner in the

7

business, well Ralph could just jump in the lake. I was sick of him.

I went up to my bedroom and shut the door. I made up a big speech about how I was never, never going to be a partner in Ralph's funeral business.

After about an hour there was a knock on the door. Ralph stuck his head in the room. He didn't say anything about the giraffe. He shook an old jar at me. I could see a coin rattling around in the bottom. 'Would you sell me one of the pennies from your coin collection?' he asked. 'I've only got one left.'

'What do you want it for?' I said suspiciously.

'They are hard to get. This jar used to be full but now I only have one left. Ever since they changed to decimal currency it has got harder and harder to get pennies. I can't use cent coins – they are too small.'

A nasty thought came into my mind. 'Has this got anything to do with the funeral business? Because if it has you are not getting any of my coins. I'm fed up with you and your dead bodies.'

'I have a man waiting for burial. Every corpse has to have two pennies. One for each eye. The spirits of the dead have no rest if they are buried without their coins.'

I picked up a pillow and threw it at him. 'Buzz off,' I yelled. 'I don't ever want to hear anything about your rotten burials again. And get it into your skull. I am never going to work for you as an undertaker – never.' Ralph's sad face disappeared from the room.

A bit later I went downstairs. I could hear Ralph talking to Mum. I can't remember the exact words but he said something like this: 'I'll leave the body in the

8

workshop for tonight. I'm too tired to move it at the moment.'

My head started to spin. This was just too much. It was the last straw. Now he had gone and brought a corpse to our home. He was leaving a dead body in the workshop for some reason or another. And he had promised me that he never would. I grabbed the key and charged down the back yard to the workshop. I opened the door and rushed inside, leaving the key in the lock.

I looked around and sure enough, just as I suspected, there on the table was a new coffin. The lid was firmly closed. Ralph didn't shut the coffin lids unless there was a body inside. Boy, was I mad. I turned around just in time to see the wind blow the door shut.

Immediately I found myself in the dark. It was pitch black. I stumbled over to the door and tried to open it. It wouldn't budge. Ralph had fitted a new deadlock after Andy had taken the coffin out for a sail. I was locked in. I couldn't even turn the light on because the switch was outside.

I yelled at the top of my voice and banged on the door as hard as I could. It was no use. No one heard me. After a while I slumped on the floor. I was exhausted. It was as quiet as the grave. I could hear my own heart thumping inside my chest. I was all alone in the darkness.

Or was I?

In the middle of the room was a coffin. With a corpse in it. I started to wonder who it was. Could it be the person who Ralph had wanted the extra penny for? Was there a body in there with one lonely penny on one of its eyes? What had Ralph said? The spirit would not rest without the pennies. And it was my fault. I wouldn't give

9

him one of mine because I was mad about the giraffe.

I sat there in the silence and the blackness. My breath sounded as loud as a windstorm. I tried to breathe quietly. I didn't want to wake the dead.

I started to think about ghosts. I imagined a ghost with one eye leering at me. Coming to claim me. I told myself not to be silly. The dead didn't come back to life, I knew that. The trouble was, that sort of advice is fine when it is daytime and all your friends are about. But when you are locked in a dark, silent room with a corpse it is quite another thing.

The silence deepened. It grew cold and I started to shiver. I was too terrified to move in case the corpse heard me. I could imagine the eye without the penny. Was it swivelling? Was it seeking me?

Then something happened which froze my blood. I heard, quite distinctly, a soft sneeze.

There was no doubt about it. A sneeze had come from inside the coffin. The corpse was alive.

I almost shrieked with fear, but somehow I managed to keep control of myself. I shoved my fist into my mouth and crouched lower in the corner. Had it been my imagination? Had I really heard a sneeze? I knew I had. I strained my ears in the silence. What was that? A scratching noise. Coming from the coffin. It was trying to get out.

'Merciful heavens,' I mumbled, 'Don't let it get me.' The scratching grew louder.

What a fool I'd been. If only I'd given Ralph that penny when he wanted it. Then the body would have lain in peace.

10

'Please come Ralph,' I whispered under my breath. 'Please come and save me.'

A wail came from the coffin.

'I'll do anything Ralph. I'll be your partner. I promise. I swear that if you come now I'll join you in the business. But just come and save me.'

At the very moment, as if he had heard my words, Ralph opened the door and came in. The room was filled with light. 'Hello,' he said. 'What are you doing here?'

I pointed at the coffin. 'It's alive,' I croaked. 'The body is alive. Save me and I'll be your partner.'

The smile vanished from his face. He walked over to the coffin and lifted up the lid. 'He is too,' he said. 'He's still breathing. 'Mrs Trapp *will* be pleased.'

'Mrs Trapp,' I managed to gasp. 'What's she got to do with it?'

'Well,' grinned Ralph as he lifted out the furry bundle, 'Fibble is her favourite cat.'

SANTA CLAWS

'I've never seen anything like it before,' said the hypnotist. 'You say he had a perfectly normal mouth yesterday?'

'Yes,' said Mrs White, looking at the tiny hole in the middle of her son's face. 'A perfectly ordinary mouth just like anyone else. Now look at it. It's so small there is only just enough room to poke in one pea at a time. The only food he can get into his mouth is soup sucked up through a straw. He can't talk, he can't stick out his tongue and he can't eat.'

A squeaky, gobbling noise came out of Sean's little mouth hole. 'What did he say?' asked the hypnotist.

'He said he can't kiss either. He won't be able to kiss his girlfriend.'

The hypnotist bent over and had another look. 'Incredible,' he said. 'You couldn't even push a pencil through that little opening. I'm surprised a straw fits in. Are you sure you don't know how it happened?'

Sean nodded his head up and down vigorously.

'He has no idea,' said Mrs White. 'He can't remember

12

anything about it at all. He just doesn't know what happened.'

'I don't normally work on Christmas Day,' said the hypnotist. 'But this is different. This is an emergency. What can I do to help?'

'We must find out where Sean's lips have gone,' answered Mrs White anxiously. 'The doctors won't do anything until they find out what happened. But how is he going to tell us? He can't talk.'

Mrs White pulled out a sheaf of paper and a Biro. 'He is very good at writing. I thought he might write it down for us.'

The hypnotist slapped his knee enthusiastically. 'It might work,' he said. 'It just might work. Come and sit at the desk, Sean. We will see what you can remember.'

The hypnotist was very happy. He had never heard of a case of a lost mouth before. He decided he would write this one up. Everyone would be interested in the case of the boy with the smallest mouth in the world.

'Close your eyes,' he said to Sean in a dreamy voice. 'And take five deep breaths. At the end of the fifth breath you will open your eyes . . . You will remember what happened to your mouth . . . You will pick up the pen and write the whole thing down . . . The whole story . . . Right from the beginning . . .'

Sean closed his eyes and took five deep breaths. On the fifth breath he opened his eyes and picked up the pen. This is what he wrote.

It all started on Christmas Eve. I had to look after my little brat of a brother. 'Take him into Myer's and show him the Christmas windows,' said Mum. 'Keep him busy for about two hours while Helen and I wrap up his

13

Christmas presents. We don't want him to see us wrapping them up, do we? After all, he still believes in Santa Claus.'

'But Mum, why can't Helen do it?' I said. 'I hate taking him shopping. He's a real pain. He gets lost and he won't do what he's told. It's Christmas Eve and I want to go and see my new girlfriend.'

'Your own brother comes before girlfriends,' she answered. 'And Helen is helping me wrap up the presents. Now off you go and don't give me any more arguments.'

It was no use. I had to go. I took Robert's hand and dragged him out to the tram stop. We lived in Fitzroy and it was only four stops on the tram to Myer's. Robert sat there sucking this dirty big icy pole with loud slurping noises. Everyone in the tram was looking at us. How embarrassing. I tried to pretend I wasn't with him but he kept asking me stupid questions like, 'How come you've got pimples on your chin, Sean?'

After what seemed like ten years we finally got to Myer's. 'I want to go and see Santa Claus,' whined Robert.

'No way,' I told him. 'I'm going to the record bar and that's that.' I grabbed him by the scruff of the neck and pulled him up to the record bar. I wanted to buy a couple of records. My favourite singers are Madonna and Sally Fritz. I have a very sexy poster of Sally Fritz at home on my bedroom wall. Mum doesn't like it. She says it's not very nice.

I didn't have time to buy a Sally Fritz record though. As soon as we got there Robert started up again. 'Santa Claus. I wanna see Santa Claus.'

14

'No,' I said.

'If you don't take me to Santa I'll pee on the floor,' he yelled.

'You wouldn't,' I said. 'Not in front of all these people.' I looked around. The place was packed out with people doing their last minute Christmas shopping.

'I will so too,' he shouted at the top of his voice. He started to lift up the leg of one side of his short trousers. People were looking. I went pale. He was going to do it. He was really going to do it with all of Melbourne watching.

'You win,' I said weakly. 'I'll take you to see Santa.' We walked across to the lifts and squeezed in with the rest of the crowd. The lift stopped at the fifth floor and everyone except us got out.

'I think Santa is on the roof garden,' I told Robert.

'He better be,' was all Robert said.

The doors opened and we stepped out into the black night. The whole place had changed. There was no roof garden and no Santa. There weren't even any lights. 'It looks like it's different this year,' I told Robert. 'Santa must be on a different level.'

'You tricked me,' he screamed. 'You tricked me. I'm telling Mum. I'm dobbing on you. You promised to take me to see Santa.'

He really was a brat. I was sick of the whole thing. Why did I always have to get stuck with him? 'There isn't any Santa Claus,' I blurted out. 'It's only an old man dressed up with a cotton wool beard and a pillow stuffed down his shirt. There's no such person as Santa Claus.'

'There is,' he screamed. 'There is, there is, there is.' He

15

started stamping his foot on the ground. Then he turned and ran back to the lift. He jumped in just as the doors were closing. He was gone.

I rushed over to the closed doors. I had to find him and quick. If he went home alone Mum would murder me. I pushed the button on the wall and waited. That's when I heard the voice. A high, squeaky voice. 'Help,' it said. 'Help me. I can't hold on much longer.'

I looked around but I couldn't see anyone. 'Over here,' squeaked the voice. 'Over on the edge.' I ran over to the edge of the building. A steel rail ran all the way around to stop people falling over. I still couldn't see anything. Then I noticed a hand hanging on to one of the rails. Someone was dangling over the edge of the building. And we were six storeys up. I looked again at the hand – there was something strange about it. It wasn't an ordinary hand. It was a very hairy hand with claws on the end. Long, bent claws like those of a lion.

I peered over the edge and could just make out a dark figure hanging on for grim death. 'Here,' I said. 'Take my hand.' Another clawed hand grasped mine and I heaved the panting figure over the edge. It fell gasping to the floor.

'Thank you,' said the squeaky voice. 'You have just saved the life of Santa Claws number 16,543.'

I peered at the queer little man who stood before me. He was short with a grubby face and dirty tangled beard that might once have been white. He was wearing a faded Santa Claus outfit which had a big hole in the pants. But the strangest thing about him were the claws on his hands. He held up his hands and extended the

16

claws. They were long and sharp. He could have ripped my ear off with them if he wanted. 'Santa Claws,' he said again. 'Number 16,543.'

I grinned. 'You've got it wrong,' I said. 'It's spelt C-l-a-U-s, not C-l-a-W-s.

The little man sighed. 'Yes, they've changed it. It should be spelt with a "w" but they thought it frightened the children. Nothing is the same these days.'

I started to laugh. 'Santa with claws. That's a good one. What would Santa want claws for?'

He looked cross. He didn't like me laughing at him. 'How do you think we get up all those chimneys?' he said. 'We have evolved claws just like giraffes have evolved long necks. We need the claws for scrambling up the chimneys.'

'We,' I said. 'What do you mean, "we"? There is only supposed to be one Santa and he certainly doesn't look like you.'

'Rubbish,' he replied. 'How could one Santa possibly get down all those chimneys on one night? There are millions of us.'

'Well, how come you're so grotty then?' I asked. Boy, this bloke was really a nut. I decided to humour him. He might be dangerous.

'You try scrambling up and down chimneys in the middle of the night and see how clean you stay,' he said hotly.

I decided to leave. I didn't want that little brat Robert getting home before me and telling Mum that I said there was no such person as Santa Claus. She wouldn't like that very much at all. I turned round and headed for the lift. Santa Claws came with me. The lift opened and

17

we both stepped in. 'Where are you going?' I asked him.

'Home with you. You saved the life of a Santa Claws and now I have to reward you.'

'Think nothing of it,' I said. 'I don't need a reward.'

I didn't want this grubby, peculiar little clawed person walking around town with me.

'I have to give you your reward. It's the rules,' he insisted. 'You saved my life and now you and all the children in your family get two wishes each. Anything you want.'

This bloke was mad. I looked at his claws again. With one swipe he could rip my hair off. I didn't answer. I was too scared. The lift went straight down to the ground floor and we stepped out into the busy shop. I walked quickly, hoping he would get lost but no such luck. He stuck to me like glue. People were looking at us and whispering to each other but Santa Claws didn't seem to notice.

'Your fly is open,' I told him. 'Do your fly up for heaven's sake.' He bent over and pulled up his zip with one of his claws.

A lady with blue hair came bustling up to us. 'Shameful,' she said angrily. 'Disgusting. How can you walk around in front of all these children with that filthy Santa's outfit? How can they believe in Santa when you look like that?'

Just then the shop Santa came walking along with a sackful of toys over his shoulder. He had a huge woolly beard and shiny vinyl boots. My Santa waved to him. The shop Santa didn't wave back. People were starting to

18

boo and shout at us. 'Let's get out of here,' I said. 'You're making a lot of trouble.'

We ran out of Myer's and jumped onto the tram. Santa Claws sat next to me. Everyone in the tram stared at us the whole way back. Santa was smelly. Even his breath smelled and he had yellow teeth. 'Don't they have toothbrushes at the North Pole?' I asked sarcastically.

Claws looked offended but he didn't say anything. When the conductor came I had to pay Claws' fare. He didn't have any money. 'Left it in the sleigh,' he said. 'When I made that forced landing at Myer's.'

Mrs White and the hypnotist snatched at each page as Sean finished writing it. 'Astonishing,' cried the hypnotist. 'Absolutely astonishing.'

Sean continued scribbling away still in a trance.

We finally reached home and I opened the front door. 'Goodbye,' I said to the grubby little Santa. 'You enter by the chimney, I believe.'

To my amazement Claws pushed past me into the lounge room. Mum was out but my big sister Helen and Robert were sitting under the Christmas tree. Robert was crying with large fake tears. 'There he is,' he yelled pointing at me. 'He said there was no Santa. He said Santa was fake.'

Then Helen started in. 'What a mean thing, Sean. Fancy telling a little boy there is no Santa. And on Christmas Eve too. And don't think that bringing that horrible little person here will make things better. Where did you get your outfit?' she said to Claws. 'At the tip?'

19

'I am in a hurry,' said Claws. 'I have a lot more homes to visit tonight. You have two wishes each. Now quickly, you first, Sean.'

I looked at those claws. They were sharp enough to rip my face off. I decided to humour him. 'Sally Fritz,' I said. 'She is my favourite rock star. Bring Sally Fritz here for a visit.'

In a flash Sally Fritz stood before us. She held a microphone in her hand and was dressed in fishnet stockings, high-heeled shoes, lace panties and a blouse you could almost see through. She must have been in the middle of a concert before Claws produced her in front of us. Her eyes were staring wide. She couldn't work out what had happened. One minute she was on stage in New York and the next she was in an Australian lounge room with three kids and a scruffy little Santa looking at her.

'Repulsive,' said Helen. 'Mum will kill you for bringing someone like that here.'

Sally Fritz put her hands up to her mouth. Then she started to scream at the top of her voice. She was scared out of her wits. 'Quick,' I yelled at Claws. 'Get rid of her.' Sally Fritz vanished without a trace, just as quickly as she had arrived.

'Well, that's your two wishes gone,' said Claws. He looked at Robert. 'What's your first wish, lad? What do you want for Christmas?'

'A machine gun,' yelled Robert. 'A real machine gun.'

A grey, steel machine gun materialised in Robert's hands. It was the most real looking machine gun I had ever seen. With a cry of joy Robert pulled the trigger. Bullets spat out with a deafening roar. They drilled holes

20

across the floor, up the walls and across the ceiling. We all dived for cover behind the sofa. When the noise stopped the room was filled with bitter blue smoke. And the room was in ruins. There were smashed ornaments and pieces of plaster all over the room.

'Look,' gasped Helen. 'Mum's grandfather clock. It's smashed to smithereens. You're in big trouble, Robert. Mum will skin you alive for this.'

Robert started to cry. He always cried when he thought he was in trouble. 'I don't want it,' he yelled at Claws. 'I wish I never had it.'

The gun disappeared and the room and the clock returned to normal. 'That's your two wishes gone,' he said to Robert. Claws looked at Helen. 'Now it's your turn. What are your two wishes my girl?'

Helen stamped her foot in temper. 'I don't like you,' she shouted. 'I wish none of us had ever heard of you.'

Suddenly we were alone in the room. Claws was gone. We all looked at each other. None of us could remember what had happened. We had no memories of Claws at all. He had wiped them all out. But for some reason I can remember it now.

The hypnotist was reading over Sean's shoulder. He nodded his head smugly. 'The trance,' he said to Mrs White excitedly. 'He remembers because of the trance.'

Sean continued writing furiously without saying a word. Not that he could with a mouth the size of a small marble.

Well, that's about the end of the story. I still don't know how I got my small mouth.

21

Helen was looking around the room. She couldn't even remember that Claws had been there and promised her two wishes. 'I feel as if someone was here,' she said. 'But I can't remember who it was or what happened.'

'Me too,' I said. 'I feel as if someone was talking to us. It had something to do with Santa Claus.'

I wished I hadn't said that. It reminded Robert of what happened at Myer's. He pointed a finger at me and started up again with the phoney tears. 'You said there was no Santa,' he yelled. 'You said he had cotton wool for a beard and a pillow down his shirt.'

Robert started jumping up and down and screaming. Then he ran out of the room and slammed the door.

Helen was mad at me. 'That was mean of you, Sean,' she said. 'You shouldn't have told him there was no Santa. I wish you didn't have such a big mouth.'

A DOZEN BLOOMIN' ROSES

See, this kid was hanging around outside the flower shop and Jenny (the shop assistant) thought he was a trouble maker. She reckoned he might be going to nick something. That's why she called for me. I have a black belt in judo and if I do say so myself I am quite good in a fight.

Not that I'm tough. No, generally I am as quiet as a lamb. I'm not big either. In fact a lot of people think I am about fourteen years old and they are amazed when I tell them I am really seventeen. I got the job at the flower shop because of my strength. They needed someone strong who could lump all the boxes around and lift heavy flower pots for Jenny. At first they didn't want me on account of my size but when they saw what I could do they changed their minds and gave me the job.

Anyway, to get back to the story. This kid (who looked about my age) really was acting strangely. He would peer into the shop looking at the flowers for sale. When anyone looked at him he sloped off down the street. About five minutes later, back he would come. This happened about twenty times. I should add that I thought I had seen him hanging around before. Perhaps on the train.

'Don't worry,' I said to Jenny. 'I'll fix this weirdo up in no time at all.' I walked out of the door and approached the boy who was acting so strangely. Straight away he turned round and started to walk off.

'Come back here,' I ordered in my sternest voice. 'I want to talk to you.' He turned around and went red in the face. I could see that he was nervous. His knees were wobbling like jelly and he just stood there with his mouth dangling open.

'What are you hanging around here for?' I asked. I started to feel sorry for him, he looked so nervous. I had a feeling that maybe he was a bit sweet on Jenny. I have to admit that she is the spunkiest girl in all of Melbourne and he wouldn't have been the first one who fancied her.

He seemed to have trouble talking. It was as if he was being strangled by invisible hands but finally he managed to gasp out the word 'flowers'.

I grabbed his arm firmly and led him in to the shop counter. 'Here,' I said giving a wink to Jenny. 'This gentleman wants flowers.'

Jenny turned on her fatal smile and said in her sweetest voice, 'What sort of flowers, Sir?'

I grinned to myself. She always called the shy ones 'Sir'. It made them feel better when they were embarrassed about buying flowers. The poor kid went even redder and looked around wildly. He obviously didn't know a kangaroo paw from a carnation. 'Roses,' he blurted out, pointing to our most expensive line.

24

I should tell you here what I found out later, at the funeral. This poor boy had twenty-six dollars in his pocket. Twenty of it was the change from his grandmother's pension cheque and six of it was his own. His grandmother needed this money badly to buy her week's groceries. Jenny looked at the roses. 'A good choice,' she said. 'They're beautiful, aren't they? How many would you like?'

Once again he struggled for words. 'How much, er, well, I, you see.' Boy, he was the shyest person I had ever seen. He just couldn't seem to get anything out. Finally the words 'one dozen' managed to escape from his frozen mouth.

Jenny started to wrap up the roses. She always goes to a lot of trouble to make them look good. She wraps the stems up in pretty paper and then she gets a long length of ribbon and ties a bow. Next she runs one of her long slender fingernails along the ends of the ribbon and they curl up like magic. I have tried to do this myself many times but it never works. Probably because I bite my fingernails.

'Are they for your girlfriend?' asked Jenny. She is a bit on the nosey side, is Jenny. The red-faced boy shook his head and looked at his shoes.

'They are for a girl though, aren't they?'

He nodded unhappily.

'Is this the first time you have given flowers to a girl?' she asked gently.

He nodded again and made a gurgling noise in his throat.

'What shall I write on the card?' I could see that Jenny felt sorry for this kid. She was trying to help him all she could. The poor thing couldn't seem to talk at all. 'What about your name,' she suggested. 'You will have to put who they are from.'

'Gerald,' he answered at last. 'My . . . my name's Gerald.'

Jenny smiled. 'And who are they for?' she asked kindly.

He didn't know which leg to stand on. He was really embarrassed. He looked at me as if he wished I wasn't there.

'Go away,' said Jenny. 'You are embarrassing a customer.'

She was the boss so I went up to the back of the shop and started stacking up some heavy concrete pots.

Jenny wrote something on the card and tied it on to the ribbon. I snuck along behind a row of daffodils so that I could hear what happened. I really hoped that things would work out well for this shy boy.

Jenny put the finishing touches to the bunch and passed over the flowers. 'Now,' she went on. 'They are two dollars each. That will be twenty-four dollars.'

Forget about Gerald being red in the face before. That was nothing to what happened next. He went as red as the dozen bloomin' roses he had just bought. This great wave of redness swept down from his ears, down his neck and for all I know right down to his toes.

Jenny and I didn't know what was the matter. It was only later I found out that he thought flowers were about two dollars a bunch at the most. He had got Jenny to wrap up the flowers and now he couldn't ask her to take them back. He was too embarrassed. He pulled his grandmother's pension money out of his pocket, looked

26

at it frantically, then thrust it into Jenny's hand. For a minute I thought he was going to say something to me. I tried to look as if I hadn't been listening. He took a few steps towards me, then, changing his mind, grabbed his change and fled out of the shop.

'What a strange bloke,' I said. 'I bet we never see him again.'

I was wrong. Half an hour later he got into the same carriage as me on the train.

I groaned. Not because of Gerald and his flowers but because Scouse the skinhead was in my carriage. He was a great big hulk of a bloke and he was real mean into the bargain. He liked nothing better than picking on someone weak and giving them a hard time. He always caught the same train as me but usually I managed to get into another carriage. He looked at Gerald, gave a twisted sneer and then spat on the floor.

Gerald was as red as ever and he stood with his back to the door, holding the flowers behind his back. He was trying to hide them from the other passengers. He didn't want to be seen carrying flowers in the train. Every now and then he looked over at me in an agitated fashion.

The train was one of those silver ones where the two doors slide automatically into the middle when they close. As the train lurched off they shut with a bang. Right on Gerald's roses. He just stood there shivering and twitching and holding onto the stems with his hands behind his back as if nothing had happened. The stems were on the inside of the train and the flowers were on the outside.

Everyone on the train started to grin. I bit my tongue like mad to stop myself from smiling but I have to admit

27

that it really was funny. Gerald just looked at a spot on the roof and stood there with his hands behind his back, pretending that nothing had happened.

A few people started twittering and giggling. The poor kid just didn't know what to do so he just kept on pretending that everything was all right. Gerald looked around desperately. I'm sure that if the door had been open he would have jumped out of the moving train just to escape from the mirth.

The only person in the train who hadn't noticed the flowers was Scouse. He was too busy scratching his shaved head and taking swigs out of a tinny. Every now and then he would give a loud burp.

The train plunged into a tunnel and for a few seconds everything was black. I stopped biting my tongue and allowed myself a big grin. I just couldn't help it. Anyway, Gerald couldn't see me smiling in the dark. Right at that moment the lights switched on and Gerald looked into my eyes.

He had seen me grinning. His bewildered eyes seemed to say, 'Not you too.' It was at this moment that I realised I had betrayed him. I forced the smile from my face and opened my mouth to speak but he looked away just as the train stopped at an underground station.

The doors slid apart and Gerald stared at what was left of his twenty-four-dollar bunch of flowers. They had gone. He stood there lamely holding twelve broken stems wrapped in pink paper. There was not one petal left. They had all been ripped off in the tunnel. Now he had lost his grandmother's money and his flowers. And even worse he had made a fool of himself in front of a whole carriage full of people including me.

28

With a strangled cry he jumped off onto the platform. Scouse jumped after him. 'Look at the little fairy clutching his invisible flowers,' sneered Scouse.

I stepped off the train too and stood aside as it sped past me.

Scouse snatched the rose stems from Gerald's hand gleefully. 'Look at this,' he mocked as he read the card that Jenny had written:

TO SAMANTHA WITH LOVE FROM GERALD.

'I'll bet she likes getting these.' He shoved the prickly stems into Gerald's face.

Gerald grabbed the broken stalks and looked around like a hunted rabbit. He looked straight at me, red with shame. He wanted to escape but Scouse was blocking his way. Without a sound, Gerald jumped off the platform onto the tracks and ran up the tunnel.

'Come back!' I shouted. 'Trains come through the loop every five minutes.'

He made no reply and I heard his clattering feet disappear into the tunnel.

'Let the little fairy go,' said Scouse showing his yellow teeth in a leer. Then he spat into my face and walked off laughing.

I ran screaming down the platform to find a porter. 'There's a boy in the tunnel!' I yelled. 'Stop the trains.'

The ground began to tremble gently and a rush of cold air came out of the tunnel. There was a low rumble and then a scream.

The train rushed out of the tunnel. As it slowed I

noticed a bunch of broken flower stems wedged on one of the buffers.

There were not many people at Gerald's funeral. Apart from the priest and the undertakers there was just me and Gerald's grandmother. After the coffin had been lowered into the ground we walked slowly back to the gate. I told the old lady about what happened in the flower shop. She already knew the rest from the police. She smiled sadly and explained about her pension money that he had spent. 'Not that I care about that,' she said. 'If only I had Gerald back I would give everything I have.'

I watched with tears in my eyes as the bent old lady slowly walked off. I had told her about that ratbag Scouse but I didn't mention that I had smiled in the train when the roses got caught in the door. I felt too ashamed.

That night I had terrible dreams about roses and thorns. I kept seeing a dark tunnel from which a lonely voice sadly called my name.

It was no better that day at work. I kept dropping things and breaking them. And the palm of my hand was itchy. I kept scratching it but nothing would stop the itch.

I was glad when it was time to knock off. I went out into the potting shed to get my parka. A terrible feeling of sadness suddenly swept over me. It seemed to flow out into my body from the palm of my left hand.

And then it happened. From the palm of my left hand a blood red rose erupted from my flesh. Slowly, it unfolded, budded and bloomed. A magnificent flower

30

nodding gently on the end of a graceful stem. I tried to scream but nothing came out. I shook my head wildly and my rose fell to the ground.

I fell in a chair dazed and watched with horror, no, not horror: awe, as eleven more perfect blooms grew from the palm of my hand.

I knew after the third one that there would be a dozen. A dozen bloomin' roses. Blood-red and each with two dots on each perfect petal. And under the dots a downturned line.

I stared at the dots. They were eyes. Unhappy eyes. And underneath, a sad little suggestion of a mouth. Each petal of each rose held a portrait of the dead boy's face. I knew that Gerald had sent me a message from beyond the grave.

I collected the roses in a daze and took them into the shop. Then I wrapped them in pink paper and tied them up with a bow. I ran a chewed fingernail along the ends and curled them up. After that I wrote on a small card and attached it to the ribbon.

Then I set off for home.

Scouse was on the train.

He leered as soon as he saw me. I stood with my back to the sliding doors and as they slid closed I let the roses become trapped in the door. I stood there, saying nothing as the train lurched off.

There was no one in the carriage except Scouse. 'Another little person with flowers in the door,' he mocked. He stood up and poked me in the stomach. It hurt. 'Another sap. Another creep who buys flowers.'

I grabbed his wrist with my one free hand and tried to stop him jabbing me.

31

Just at that moment the train plunged into the tunnel and Scouse broke my hold in the blackness. I felt his powerful arms on my neck and I fought desperately for breath. I was choking. He was strangling me.

I felt my life ebbing away but I just couldn't bring myself to let go of those roses and so I only had one free hand and couldn't stop him.

Without warning the doors burst apart as if opened by giant arms. A roaring and rushing filled the carriage. A sweet smell of roses engulfed us. The hands released my neck and Scouse screamed with terror. As the light flicked on I saw that the compartment was filled with rambling roses. They twisted and climbed at astonishing speed. They covered the luggage racks and the safety rails. They twisted along the seats and completely filled the compartment. I couldn't move. Then I saw that the long tendrils wound around Scouse's leg and arms. And neck.

Tighter and tighter they drew around the hapless man's throat until at last he lay still on the floor. I knew that he was dead.

And then, as quickly as they had come, the creeping roses snaked out of the door and vanished into the black tunnel. There was not a sign that they had ever been there. Except the one dozen roses that I had started with. They were perfectly intact. Not damaged a bit by their exposure to the tunnel. I smoothed down my dress and then picked up the bunch of roses as the train stopped at the station.

I looked again at the label I had written. It said:

TO GERALD WITH LOVE FROM SAMANTHA.

When I got home Mum was amazed by the roses. 'Why Samantha,' she said. 'They are beautiful. And look, each petal has two little dots that look like eyes and a little line like a mouth. They are faces.'

I could feel tears forming in my eyes. 'Yes,' I said, examining them closely. 'And each little face is smiling.'

TONSIL EYE 'TIS

Good grief. I am gone. I have had it. That good looking girl from next door has seen me pulling the hairs out of my nose. She thinks I am grotty. Now I will have to tell her the whole story because I can see by the look on her face that she is disgusted. I have already lost Tara, my girlfriend. I couldn't stand it if Jill gets the wrong idea too.

'Listen, Jill. Don't look like that. There is a very good reason why I do it. You don't think I like pulling the hairs out of my nose do you? It is very painful.'

Jill is not saying anything. She is just staring at me so I go on with the story. 'This little garden gnome business is only here because of my nose-hair pulling. You don't believe me? Well look at this.'

I take my hand off the new garden gnome's head and show her the eye that has grown on the end of my finger. I have never shown anyone this little eye before. I can see with it, which is a fairly unusual thing. When I am not making gnomes I keep a glove on so that no one can see the eye. Jill's mouth is hanging open with surprise so I

34

decide to tell her about the way the whole thing happened before she thinks I have gone crazy.

It all begins when my girlfiend Tara gives me a garden gnome for my fourteenth birthday. It is a horrible looking garden gnome and it only has one eye. 'It's lovely,' I say to Tara. 'Just what I wanted. A little angry looking garden gnome.'

It is angry looking, too. Its one and only eye glares at everyone as if its toenails are being pulled out. And its mouth is wide open like someone yelling out swear words at the footy. It is made out of cement but it is very realistic.

'I am so glad you like it,' says Tara in a dangerous voice. 'Because it cost me a lot of money.'

'I can see that,' I answer. 'Anyone can tell that it is a very special garden gnome. I know just the spot for it – down behind the garden shed.'

'Behind the garden shed,' yells Tara. 'You can't put it out in the rain. I don't think you like it.'

'I was only joking,' I say quickly. 'I will put it on the shelf where I can see it all the time.'

So that is how the garden gnome comes to be in my bedroom. Every morning and every night there it is glaring at me. As the days go by it seems to look grumpier and grumpier.

After a while I find that I can't sleep at night. The angry gnome gets into my dreams. I wake up at night and find that I can't stop staring at its horrible little face. I keep having a nightmare about being swallowed by it.

I turn the gnome around so that it faces the wall but

35

this does not work either. I keep imagining that it is pulling faces. Finally I can stand it no more. I grab the gnome by its silly little red hat and am just about to smash it to smithereens when I notice something strange. Inside its mouth, right at the back, is a tiny little face about half the size of a pea. It is stuck on the gnome's tonsils.

I think that whoever made this garden gnome has a strange sense of humour. I decide to remove the little face from the gnome's tonsils. I get a small hammer and a screwdriver and I start chipping away at the little face at the back of the gnome's throat. I feel a bit like a dentist. The gnome's mouth is wide open but I bet he would close it if he could.

After a couple of hits the little face flies off the gnome's tonsils and falls onto its tongue.

The next bit is hard to believe but it really does happen. The little round face rolls along the garden gnome's concrete tongue, onto its lips and flies through the air. It hits me full in the mouth. 'Ouch,' I yell at the top of my voice. 'That hurt.'

It is so painful that my eyes start to water. I am really mad now and I start searching around on the carpet for the little round face. It is nowhere to be seen. I search and search but I can't find it anywhere. My lips are still hurting and I have a funny, tickling feeling somewhere at the back of my throat.

'Right,' I yell at the gnome. 'You have had it.' I pick up the screwdriver and throw it as hard as I can. The point of the screwdriver hits the gnome on his one and only eye and knocks it clean out of his face. Now the gnome

36

has no eyes at all. It is lucky it is only made out of concrete or it would be a very unhappy gnome.

I look around the floor for the eye but I can't find that either. This is when I notice that one of my fingers on my right hand is feeling sore.

What happens next is really weird. I find myself looking up at my own face. It is just as if I am lying on the carpet looking up at myself. I am looking down and up at the same time. My head starts to swim. I feel I must be having a nightmare. I hope I am having a nightmare because if not I must be going nuts. There on the end of one of my fingers, is a little eye. A real eye. It is staring and blinking and I can see with it.

The gnome's eye has somehow grown onto my finger.

I give a scream of rage and fear and then I grab the gnome and run outside with it. I throw it down onto the path and smash it to pieces with the hammer. By the time I am finished all that is left is a small pile of dust and powder.

The gnome is gone for good but the eye is not. No, the eye is still there, blinking and winking on the end of my finger. I shove my hand in my pocket because I can't bear to look at my extra eye. Suddenly I can see what is in my pocket. There is a used tissue, two cents (which is all the money I have in the world) and a half-sucked licorice block. The eye is looking around inside my pocket.

I grin. At first I think that maybe this is not too bad. An extra eye on the end of a finger might be useful. I go back to my bedroom and poke my finger into a little hole in the wall. There is a family of mice nesting there. They get a big fright when they see the finger-eye looking at them and they nick off as fast as they can go.

Next I stick my finger into my earhole to see what is going on in there. My new eye seems to be able to see in the dark, but to be quite honest, there is not really much action inside an ear.

This is when I get the idea to have a peek inside my own mouth. I have always wondered what it is like at the back of my throat and this is my big chance to find out. I poke my finger in and have a look around. It is quite interesting really, I have never seen behind that thing that dangles down at the back before. There are a lot of red, wet mountains back there.

Suddenly I see something terrible. Horrible. A little face is staring back at me. It is the little, round face that I chipped off the gnome's tonsils. It has taken up residence in my throat. It lives behind my tonsils.

I start to cough and splutter. I have to get it out. Fancy having a little round face living in your throat. I try everything I can think of to get it out (including blowing my nose about a thousand times) but it just will not come out.

'Okay,' I say. 'If you will not come out by force I will get you out with brains.' I go down to the kitchen to see what there is to eat. I notice a packet of Hundreds and Thousands that Mum uses to sprinkle on top of cakes.

'Just the right size,' I say to myself. I put three of the Hundreds and Thousands on my tongue and put my finger up to my mouth to see what happens. Sure enough, the little face rolls onto my tongue and eats two

38

of them. It eats the red ones but doesn't seem to like the blue one.

'Right,' I say. I pick out about fifteen red Hundreds and Thousands and put them on my tongue so that they form a little trail. The trail leads onto my lip and down my chin. I open my mouth and watch with the eye on my finger from a distance. The little face rolls out and starts eating. He reaches my lips and still he is not suspicious. A bit later he looks around outside and then moves down to my chin to eat the Hundreds and Thousands I have put there.

As quick as a flash I close my mouth and leave him trapped on the outside. I have won. Or so I think.

The little face tries to burrow back through my closed lips but I have my teeth clenched together. He can't get in.

I raise my hand to grab him, but before I can, he races upwards and disappears into my nose. In about two seconds I can feel him back behind my tonsils. I know that he will not fall for the Hundreds and Thousands trick again.

Just then, there is a knock at the front door. I walk down the hall and put my finger up to the keyhole to see who it is. It is Tara, my girlfriend. I open the door and give her a weak smile. 'G'day,' I say. 'How are you doing?'

'I have come to have a look at the garden gnome I gave you,' she says. 'I want to make sure that you haven't put it down the back yard.'

My heart sinks. Tara is standing next to a pile of powder and dust that is the remains of the gnome. She has not seen it yet.

39

'Come in and sit down,' I say. I try to think of an explanation but I know that I can't tell Tara. She won't like the little face on my tonsils. She certainly won't like my extra eye. Once she wouldn't go out with me just because I had a pimple on my ear. If I tell her the truth she will drop me like a brick.

I can feel the little face moving around at the back of my throat. I have to know what he is up to so I put my finger into my mouth to see what is going on.

'What are you sucking your finger for?' asks Tara.

The little face is right on the end of the dangler thing in my throat. He is swinging on it having fun.

'Take your finger out of your mouth and answer me, you silly boy,' Tara snaps.

The little face is hanging on to the dangler by his teeth! It hurts like nothing.

'Stop sucking your finger, you idiot,' yells Tara.

Now the face is out of sight. He is hiding up the back somewhere. I shove my finger in further to find out what is going on. This is a big mistake. I touch something that I shouldn't with my finger and it makes me sick. I spew up all over the carpet. Some of it splashes on Tara's shoes.

I get down onto my hands and knees and start sifting through the spew. I hope that the little face has been swept out with the tide. But it hasn't.

'You revolting creep,' yells Tara. 'I am breaking it off. You're dropped. I never want to see you again in my life.' She stands up and charges out of the door.

'Good riddance,' I yell. 'And take your rotten gnome with you. You will find what is left of it on the foot-path.'

I stagger out into the front garden and sit down. I feel

40

terrible. My life is ruined. My girlfriend has dropped me. I have no money (except for two cents). I have an eye on my finger and a little face in my throat. I wish I was dead. I start to cry. Tears fall down my face. And down my finger. The eye on my finger is shedding tears too. Little teardrops fall onto the grass.

Then something amazing starts to happen. Where the tears from my finger are falling, little concrete gnomes start to grow in the grass. I can't believe it. They are sad little gnomes but they are very life-like. They look just as if they are alive.

Ten little gnomes grow, one for each teardrop. The next day I sell the gnomes for ten dollars each. I make a hundred dollars profit.

Jill is listening to my story with wide open eyes. I don't suppose she will believe it.

'Well,' says Jill. 'What a sad tale.'

'Yes,' I answer. I can hardly believe my ears. Jill believes the whole thing. This is when I notice what a spunk she really is.

'What I can't understand,' she goes on, 'is what all this had to do with pulling hairs out of your nose.'

I feel a bit embarrassed but I decide to tell her the truth. 'I am trying to grow more gnomes,' I say. 'But I can't make any tears come. When you pull the hairs in your nose it makes your eyes water.' I hold up my finger and show her my extra eye again.

'Is the little face still there?' she asks.

'Yes.'

'And have you got any more Hundreds and Thousands?'

41

'Yes,' I answer again, handing over the packet.

'Well,' she says. 'We can't have you pulling hairs out of your nose. It's not a nice habit. Open up your mouth and let me speak to the face.'

I open my mouth and Jill looks inside and speaks to my guest. 'Listen,' she says. 'We don't mind you living in there. But fair's fair. You have to pay the rent. You help us and we will help you.'

So this is how Jill becomes my girlfriend. And we both become very rich from selling garden gnomes. We have got the perfect system. I open up my mouth and Jill calls out instructions to my tenant.

The little face goes up and pulls on a hair in my nose with his teeth. This makes my eye water and drop tears onto the lawn. More concrete gnomes grow out of the grass. Then we give the face his reward – red Hundreds and Thousands.

The gnomes are so realistic that we get five hundred dollars each for them. This means I don't have to have my hairs pulled very often.

You don't believe the story? Well, all I can say is this. If you are ever thinking of buying a garden gnome have a look in its mouth first. If there is a little face on its tonsils – don't buy it.

UNHAPPILY EVER AFTER

Albert pulled up his socks and wiped his sweaty hands on the seat of his pants. He did up the top button of his shirt and adjusted his school tie. Then he trudged slowly up the stairs.

He was going to get the strap.

He knew it, he just knew it. He couldn't think of one thing he had done wrong but he knew Mr Brown was going to give him the strap anyway. He would find some excuse to whack Albert – he always did.

Albert's stomach leapt up and down as if it was filled with jumping frogs. Something in his throat stopped him from swallowing properly. He didn't want to go. He wished he could faint or be terribly sick so he would have to be rushed off to hospital in an ambulance. But nothing happened. He felt his own feet taking him up to his doom.

He stood outside the big brown door and trembled. He was afraid but he made his usual resolution. He would not cry. He would not ask for mercy. He would not even wince. There was no way he was going to give Mr Brown that pleasure.

He took a deep breath and knocked softly.

Inside the room Brown heard the knock. He said nothing. Let the little beggar suffer. Let the little smart alec think he was in luck. Let him think no one was in.

Brown heard Albert's soft footsteps going away from the door. 'Come in, Jenkins,' he boomed.

The small figure entered the room. He wore the school uniform of short pants, blue shirt and tie. His socks had fallen down again.

Albert looked over to the cupboard where the long black strap hung on a nail.

Brown towered over Albert. He wore a three-piece suit with a natty little vest. He frowned. The wretched child showed no fear. He didn't beg, he didn't cry. He just stood there.

In the corner a grandfather clock loudly ticked away the time that lay between Albert and his painful fate. The soft 'clicks' of a cricket match filtered through the open window. Albert pretended he was out there playing with the others.

Brown suddenly thrust his hand into his vest pocket and pulled out a piece of paper. He pushed it into Albert's face. Somehow Albert managed to focus his eyes on it and see the words:

BALD HEAD BROWN WENT TO TOWN,
RIDING ON A PONY.

Underneath was a drawing of a bald-headed person riding a horse.

44

'I didn't do it, Sir,' said Albert truthfully.

Brown looked at Albert's thick black hair and wiped his hand over his own bald head. The room started to swirl, his forehead throbbed. Jenkins was lying. And he was unafraid. He should be whimpering and crawling like the others.

Brown rushed over to the cupboard and grabbed the strap. 'Hold out your hand,' he shrieked.

Then he rained blow after blow on the helpless, shaking child.

Brown sprawled in his leather chair. He was out of breath. He knew he had overdone it this time. He had lost his temper. He wondered if Jenkins would have any bruises. Some of the other teachers might kick up a fuss if Jenkins showed them bruises. Fortunately this was a boarding school and there were no parents around to complain. Brown suddenly wished he had hit Jenkins even harder. He looked out of the window at the spar-kling sea nearby. It was the perfect day to be on the water. He decided to go out in his rowing boat. It might help him to forget Jenkins and all the other little horrors in the school.

The sea was flat and mirrored the glassy clouds that beckoned from the horizon. Brown pushed out the small boat and it knifed a furrow through the inky water. He put his back to the oars and soon he was far out to sea with the shore only a thin line in the distance.

Brown was glad to be out of reach of the children he hated, but something was wrong. The sea didn't feel the same, or smell the same. He thought he heard voices – watery, giggling voices. He looked around but there was

45

not another craft to be seen. He was alone on an enamelled ocean.

The boat began to rock gently and Brown felt it gripped in a strong current. It was carrying him away from the land. He tried to turn the boat around and pull for the shore but the current was too strong. The boat sped faster and faster and then began to rock wildly. Brown felt the oars snatched from his hands by the speeding tide. He fell with a crash to the bottom of the boat and clung to the edges as it bucketed through the swirling water.

Laughter filled the still air and echoed in his head. Brown plucked up his courage and peeped over the side of the boat. It was cutting a large circle through the foam, getting neither closer nor further away from the shore.

Suddenly a piercing pain shot through Brown's head. He just had time to notice that the sea had opened up into a large funnel. The water was twirling as if it was going down a plughole. Brown collapsed into blackness as the boat slipped over the rim of the abyss.

When he awoke the pain had gone. Brown found himself still in the boat. It was speeding around the inside of the funnel at an enormous rate. He looked up at the rim and beyond that to the clouds which spun like patterns on a drunken dinner plate.

The boat maintained its position, neither falling lower in the funnel nor rising to the surface high above. Brown peered cautiously over the edge and looked down. He gasped as he saw the spiralling funnel twist down and end in jagged claws of rock which clutched hungrily upwards from the bed of the sea.

Brown found his gaze drawn into the shining black wall of the vortex. With a shock he saw a scene unfold within the sea. Two enormous lobsters were holding a struggling, naked man over a pot of boiling water. As they dropped the figure to his death, Brown was sure he heard one of them say, 'I've heard they scream as they hit the water. I don't believe it myself.'

This scene repeated itself every time the boat circled. It was like a record stuck in a groove. Brown saw it a hundred times, a thousand times. It was horrible. He didn't want to watch but his eyes were held by an unseen force. Finally he grabbed the side of the boat, closed his eyes and rocked with all his strength.

The boat slipped down a few notches. When he opened his eyes another scene unfolded. A fat man sat peering through a window at a table laden with food. Trifles, jellies, cakes, peaches and strawberries. Around the table thin, ghostly children sat stuffing themselves and laughing happily. The fat man banged on the window. He was hungry. He wanted to get in. But the children couldn't see him, couldn't hear him and the man banged in vain. He was starving – never to be satis-fied.

Brown watched, horrified as the same drama played again and again. Where was this place? Was it hell? Were these people having done to them what they had done to others? For ever? Over and over again?

Brown knew every groove would contain a similar horror. He could stand it no longer. He wanted to see no more. He decided to get it over and done with. He grabbed the sides of the boat and rocked and rocked and rocked. The boat plummeted to the waiting rocks below.

There was a tearing, crushing, splintering as Brown's last scream fled his tortured body.

Brown awoke and looked around. With relief he saw he was still in his study. The grandfather clock ticked away loudly in the corner and the soft 'clicks' of a game of cricket filtered through the open window. His leather chair rested in its usual place.

He must have had a nightmare. For a second, but only a second, he wondered if there had been some message in his terrible dream. Then he dismissed the thought and tried to think of another excuse to give Jenkins a belting. He wasn't the least bit sorry for what he had done.

It was then he noticed the room seemed different. The grandfather clock looked taller than usual and the window appeared further from the floor. Everything was bigger. He looked down and saw he was wearing short pants. And his socks were hanging down around his shoes. He was dressed in the school uniform.

And worse – oh – much worse. Albert Jenkins was in the room. A huge Jenkins. He wore a three-piece suit with a natty little vest.

Jenkins shoved a piece of paper into Brown's face. Then he rushed over to the cupboard and grabbed the strap.

SPOOKS INCORPORATED

The house was enclosed in darkness and Miss Pebble was all alone. She had been alone for sixty years. She had no family and there was no one to care for her or help her. And now she was scared. But it was no good calling out. She was alone in the night.

She loved her old house. She had lived in it all her life. She loved the old verandah and the tin roof. She loved the old cellar under the ground. She loved everything about it. It was her home.

A few days earlier a shifty looking character had offered her a lot of money for the old cottage. But Miss Pebble wouldn't sell. She wanted to live in the house until she died.

People said there was a ghost in the house. They said Ned Kelly had once lived there many years ago. Before he had been hanged for murder and robbery. Some people said that Ned's ghost walked at night. Moaning and groaning and wearing the steel armour and helmet that he had made to protect himself from the bullets of the police. Miss Pebble didn't believe it. She didn't believe the house was haunted. She had never heard any moaning in the night. Not until now.

She sat up in bed. There was someone in the house. She could hear movement. It sounded like someone crying.

The noise was coming from the kitchen. It was very soft. She told herself not to be silly, there was nothing there. It was just her nerves. But she could feel her hands shaking in the dark. She wanted to turn on the light and go and look. She knew she couldn't go to sleep until she had checked in the kitchen. But she was too scared. So she lay there all alone. In the dark.

The noise grew louder. It was coming closer, coming along the hall. Miss Pebble heard clinking. And clanking. It sounded like chains being dragged along. Something was coming towards her room. It was definitely moaning and groaning and clinking and clanking. Miss Pebble gave a little sob. She wanted to scream. She wanted to shout for help. But she didn't. She lay there saying nothing, hoping it would go away.

The noise came closer and closer.

Light appeared under the bedroom door. Soft flickering light, like light from a candle. Miss Pebble gasped. Her heart beat quickly and her head started to spin.

And then the door began to open. Slowly. Light flickered into the room. Slowly, slowly the door opened. And there in the dark hall he stood. The ghost of Ned Kelly. He had a steel helmet over his head with a slit cut out for the eyes. His chest was covered with steel plates. In one hand was a candle and in the other was a revolver. Green eyes glowed through his helmet.

Miss Pebble froze. Her heart almost stopped with fear.

Ned Kelly started to walk towards the bed. He moaned. His armour creaked. He stretched out a hand for Miss Pebble, a long, skinny hand. Then the candle went out. It was completely black.

Miss Pebble screamed. She put her hands to her mouth and screamed and screamed. Then she jumped out of bed. She stumbled through the darkness out into the hall. Out through the front door.

It was raining outside. It was freezing cold. But Miss Pebble didn't care. She ran out into the street screaming. She was soaking wet and her bare feet were cut and bleeding. She fled down the road and into the dark night.

Ned was alone in the bedroom. He walked over to the door and switched on the light. Then he looked at his watch. It was a digital watch. It said 12.45 a.m.

The figure pulled off his hood. He wasn't a Ned Kelly at all. And he wasn't a ghost. He was a young man, a teenager. He laughed to himself. 'That will make the old bag sell the house,' he said. 'Or my name is not Mick Harris.'

The next night in another town an old man was locking up a church. His name was Mr Pickle. All the others had gone. Choir practice was over. It was dark outside and cold. He put his hat on his bald head and shivered. He wished he was home, having his supper of cheese and biscuits and a nice glass of port.

He thought of the warm fire at home and his favourite

51

TV show – 'A Country Practice'. He decided to hurry back.

He took the short cut home through the graveyard. The graves were old and the grass was long. But there was a little track that went past his mother's grave. Mr Pickle looked after her grave. He kept it tidy and he put flowers on it every Sunday after church.

But tonight it was windy and cold and dark. He took his hat off as he went past his mother's grave but he kept walking. Then he stopped. Something was different. The flower bowl had gone. He turned round and went back to the grave.

The moon went behind a cloud. The night grew even darker and it was hard to see. Mr Pickle bent down and looked at the grass on the grave. His heart almost stopped. He saw something terrible. The grass moved. He was sure the grass had moved.

He took a step back. The grass on the grave was moving up and down. He was filled with horror. There was a scraping noise, like digging. Something was digging its way out of the grave. Suddenly a small hole appeared. And out of it came the bones of a hand. The skeleton of a hand and an arm appeared. And waved around. On one finger was a wedding ring.

Mr Pickle was filled with fear. He opened and closed his mouth. 'No, no,' he screamed. He took a step backwards. Then he felt a sharp pain in his chest and down his arm. He put his hand over his heart. The pain grew worse. It was killing him. He fell to the ground and lay still.

A man ran out from behind a tree. It was a fat man dressed in a suit. He bent over Mr Pickle. He put his head on Mr Pickle's chest and listened. Then he picked up Mr Pickle's arm and felt his wrist. There was no pulse.

The skeleton arm was still waving around in the hole. The man in the suit ran over to it. He pulled out the arm and threw it on the ground. A groan came out of the hole.

'Shut up Mick, you fool,' said the man. 'Pickle is dead. He's croaked it. We've gone too far this time.'

The man grabbed a shovel. He started to dig in the grave. He uncovered a long box. Then he opened the lid. A young man sat up, a teenager. 'What's up, Shifty?' he asked.

'You're a fool. That's what's up,' said Shifty. 'He's dead. Pickle is as dead as a doornail. And it's your fault.'

'It was your idea, not mine,' said the teenager.

'Listen, Mick,' said Shifty. 'I told you to get in the box. I told you to wave the skeleton hand. But I didn't tell you to put a ring on the finger. He thought it was his mother's ring. It was too much for him. It gave him a heart attack. Now he's dead.'

'Don't try to blame me,' said Mick. 'Or I'll flatten you.'

'Okay, don't get ants in your pants. Let's get out of here before someone comes.'

Shifty and Mick ran back to the road. They got into an old truck. On the side it said:

SPOOKS FOR HIRE

Mick and Shifty drove home quickly. They wanted to get away from Mr Pickle's body. They didn't want to get caught.

The two men ran a business called SPOOKS INCORPORATED.

They dressed up as ghosts to frighten people. They went to old houses that were supposed to be haunted and scared the owners so that they sold their homes. Mick and Shifty's friends bought the houses cheap, then paid the two crooks for what they had done.

'Will we get paid now that Mr Pickle is dead?' said Mick. 'We were only supposed to scare him. Not kill him.'

'Of course we'll get paid,' said Shifty. 'His house will have to be sold now. Dead men don't own houses. This has been a good week. Last night we scared the daylights out of old Miss Pebble. and tonight we knocked off Mr Pickle. We get a thousand dollars for each. Two thousand dollars for two nights' work. That's good money. Real good.'

'What's the next job?' asked Mick. 'Who do we scare next?'

'There's a pub in Melbourne called Young and Jackson's,' replied Shifty. 'It's supposed to be haunted. We are going to scare the owner into selling it for a cheap price.'

'Tell me the story about the ghost in the pub,' said Mick. 'Not that I believe in ghosts. Only fools believe in ghosts.'

'Well,' Shifty said. 'A long time ago a bloke called John Heart owned Young and Jackson's. He wanted to see if he could stop meat going bad. So he got a chicken and chopped off its head. Then he filled the chicken up with salt. He thought that filling the chicken up with salt would stop it going rotten.'

'Did it work?'

'No one knows,' said Shifty. He cut himself while he was chopping off the chook's head and the next day he died.'

'And now his ghost is supposed to haunt the pub,' said Mick.

'No,' yelled Shifty. 'The ghost of the headless chicken is supposed to haunt the pub.'

Mick and Shifty started to laugh. They both thought it was funny. Very funny indeed.

The next day Mick and Shifty made their plans. They were going to spook the owner of the pub so that he would get scared and sell it.

'How are we going to get the ghost of a headless chicken?' asked Mick. 'Dressing up as Ned Kelly was a good idea. That scared Pebble but I can't dress up as a chicken. I'm too big.'

'We are going to make one,' said Shifty. 'We are going to make a headless chicken.'

Mick and Shifty spent ten days making a mechanical chicken. They used feathers, wheels and a small motor, and they put red paint around its neck to look like blood. At last it was finished. Shifty put it on the floor. 'Terrific,' he said. 'It looks just like the real thing. The owner of the pub will be scared out of his wits.'

'Let's see if it can walk,' said Mick. 'Press the remote control.' Shifty pressed a button and the headless chicken ran around in circles. It flapped its wings and shook its headless neck. 'Wonderful,' Mick went on. 'In the dark it will look just like the real thing. The ghost of the headless chook. Something is missing, though. It's good, but it needs something else.' He looked at the mechanical chicken for a while. Then he said, 'I know. It needs to make a noise. It needs to cluck.'

'Don't be a fool. How can it cluck?' Shifty replied. 'It has no head. A chook can't cluck without a head.'

'That's all the better,' Mick told him. 'Don't you see? A chicken with no head that makes a noise is more scary. It will be more ghostly if it clucks. All we have to do is put a tape recorder inside it. You can make some clucking noises and I will put them on tape. Then we put the tape inside the chicken.'

'Great,' yelled Shifty. 'A terrific idea. You go and get a blank tape. And I'll find a small tape recorder.'

A few minutes later Shifty came back holding a cassette tape. 'I can't find a blank tape,' he said. 'But this is an old tape with folk songs on it. We can tape the chicken noises over the top.'

Mick put the tape in the recorder and pressed the RECORD button. Shifty started to cluck like a chicken.

'Wonderful,' said Mick. 'You sound just like the real thing.' After a while he stopped the tape recorder. 'That will do the trick. That should be enough clucking to scare anyone to death.'

They put the mechanical chicken on the floor and started it up. Once again it ran around in circles and flapped its wings. But this time it clucked as well. 'Fantastic,' shouted Mick. 'That tape sounds just like a chicken.'

That night Mick and Shifty crept down to Young and Jackson's pub. They waited outside. At midnight the lights went out. The back door opened. The landlord came out carrying a rubbish bin. 'This is it,' said Mick.

'This is where we give the poor sucker the fright of his life.' He put the mechanical chicken on the footpath and hid behind a fence. The chicken ran out onto the road. It flapped its wings and clucked. Red paint dripped from its neck.

The landlord just stood there holding the bin. He couldn't believe his eyes. Then he groaned. 'It's true,' he said. 'The story is true. It's the ghost of the headless chicken.' His knees knocked together. His hands shook. He tried to run but he couldn't. He was glued to the spot. The chicken kept running in circles, clucking loudly.

Mick whispered to Shifty. 'Let it go for a while. Give him a good scare. Then we might not have to come back again.' The two crooks peeped around the fence. They laughed to themselves. They thought it was a great joke. The landlord was so scared he couldn't move.

After a while Mick stepped out onto the path. He pretended he was just walking along the street. The poor landlord saw him. 'Look,' the landlord managed to say. 'The ghost of the headless chicken.'

'Where?' said Mick. 'I can't see anything.' This was a trick he often used. He pretended not to see the chicken. Even though it was flapping and clucking right in front of him.

The landlord leaned against the wall. His face was white. He looked as if he was going to faint. But before he did, something happened. The chicken started to sing. It ran around flapping its wings. And singing. It sang:

'There was a wild colonial youth,
Jack Doolan was his name;
Of poor but honest parents
He was born in Castlemaine.'

57

'You fool, Shifty,' yelled Mick. 'You didn't wipe all the folk songs off the tape.'

Shifty put his head around the corner. The chicken went quiet for a second but it kept running around. Then it started up again:

' "I'll fight but I won't surrender," said
The wild colonial boy.'

The landlord stared at the chicken. Then he stared at Mick and Shifty. 'A trick,' he yelled. 'A dirty, rotten trick.'

He ran over to the mechanical chicken and picked it up. He saw it had wheels. He threw it on the ground with an angry roar. Then he turned to Mick and Shifty. The landlord was a big man. Very big. 'I'll teach you ratbags a lesson,' he shouted. 'I'll get you for this.' Mick and Shifty turned and ran. They ran for their lives. Down the street they went. Faster and faster. But the landlord followed them. And after him came the chicken.

The landlord started to slow down. He couldn't keep up. But the chicken could. It passed him and followed Shifty and Mick down the street. It was flapping its wings and clucking its head off.

The chase went on for quite a while but eventually the landlord gave up. He shook his fist at the two men and the chicken and turned round and went back towards Young and Jackson's pub.

Mick looked over his shoulder. 'It's all right,' he puffed. 'He's gone back.' Then Mick noticed the chicken. 'Well, look at that. The stupid mechanical chicken has come after us. I thought it was supposed to run around in circles.'

They both looked at the chicken. It was flapping its wings and moving up and down on its legs. 'Hey,' yelled Shifty. 'When did you put those legs on the chicken? I didn't know it had legs.'

The headless chicken sat down on the footpath. Then it stood up. There was something underneath it. 'An egg,' screamed Shifty. 'It's laid an egg.' His eyes almost popped out of his head. He couldn't believe what he was seeing. He bent down to pick up the egg. But his fingers couldn't grab it. He couldn't pick it up. He could see right through it. The egg was transparent.

'Ahgggg,' he screamed. 'It's a ghost egg.'

'Rubbish,' shouted Mick. 'I'm sick of this.' He ran at the chicken and kicked at it. His leg passed though the chicken and he fell flat on his back. The chicken sat there clucking. It wasn't hurt at all. They both stood there looking at it. The moon came out. This time it was Mick who screamed. 'Ahgggg, I can see through it. And there's something inside it. It's salt. That's not our chicken. It's the ghost. It's the ghost of the real chicken.'

For a second they just stood there. They were too scared to move. Then the chicken flapped up onto Mick's shoulder. Little drops of blood fell from its headless neck. Both men screamed together. They turned and ran for their lives. Down the streets and through lanes they fled. And close behind followed the ghostly chicken.

At last they reached the river. Shifty was puffing. He was out of breath. 'Quick,' he grunted. 'Down here. Down these steps.' They ran down some steps that led to the Yarra River. There was a row boat at the bottom. The chicken was right behind them. They jumped into the little boat and floated out onto the river. Shifty took one oar and Mick took the other. Soon they were well out in the deep water.

'It can't follow us here,' said Mick. 'We're safe now.' But he was wrong. Sitting on the back of the boat, still clucking, was the ghost of the headless chicken. Mick stood up and started to scream.

'Sit down, you fool,' yelled Shifty. 'You're rocking the boat.' The boat started to rock from side to side. Mick grabbed at the edge. And the little boat tipped over. Mick and Shifty disappeared under the cold, black water. Neither of them could swim.

The landlord of the pub arrived home. On the footpath he found the mechanical chicken. Its battery had run out and it lay still on the footpath. He went over to the chicken and jumped up and down on it. Then he threw the broken pieces of wheels and wire into the bin.

The next morning while he was walking by the river, the landlord found two dead men in the mud.

They say that if you go down to the Yarra River on a dark night, just near Young and Jackson's pub, you will see two ghostly men in a boat. They are rowing as fast as they can. They are scared out of their wits. Because in the back of the boat sit the ghosts of two headless chickens.

One of the chickens is stuffed with salt and is clucking. The other chicken is singing 'The Wild Colonial Boy' at the top of its voice.

THE COPY

I was rapt. It was the best day of my life. I had asked Fiona to go with me and she said yes. I couldn't believe it. I mean it wasn't as if I was a great catch. I was skinny, weak, and not too smart at school. Mostly I got Cs and Ds for marks. And I couldn't play sport at all. I hated football, always went out on the first ball at cricket and didn't know which end to hold a tennis racquet. And Fiona had still said she'd be my girlfriend.

Every boy in year eleven at Hamilton High would be jealous. Especially Mat Hodson. It was no secret that he fancied Fiona too. I grinned to myself. I wished I could see his face when he found out the news. He thought that he was so great and in a way he was. He was the exact opposite to me. He was smart (always got As for everything), captain of the footy team, the best batsman in the cricket team and he was tough. Real tough. He could flatten me with one punch if he wanted to. I just hoped he took it with good grace about Fiona and me. I didn't want him for an enemy.

I headed off to Crankshaft Alley to see my old friend

61

Dr Woolley. I always went to see him when something good happened. Or something bad. I felt sort of safe and happy inside his untidy old workshop and it was fun seeing what crazy thing he was inventing. Everything he had come up with so far had been a flop. His last invention was warm clothespegs to stop people getting cold fingers when they hung out the clothes. They worked all right but no one would buy them because they cost two-hundred dollars each. All of his inventions had turned out like that. They worked and they were clever but they were too expensive for people to buy.

I walked on down past all the other little shop-front factories until I reached Dr Woolley's grubby door. I gave the secret knock (three slow, three fast) and his gnomish face appeared at the window. I say gnomish because he looked just like a gnome: he was short with a hooked nose and he had a white beard and a bald head surrounded with a ring of white hair. If you gave him a fishing rod and a red cap and sat him in the front yard you would think he was a little garden statue.

He opened the door. 'Come in Rodney,' he said.

'Tim,' I corrected. He always called me the wrong name. He had a terrible memory.

'Where's that screwdriver?' he said. 'It's always getting lost.'

'In your hand,' I told him.

'Thanks, Peter, thanks.'

'Tim,' I sighed. I don't know why I bothered. He was never going to call me by my right name. It wasn't that he didn't know who I was. He did. I was his only friend. Everyone else thought he was a dangerous crackpot because he chased them away from his front door with a

62

broken mop. I was the only person allowed into his workshop.

'Are you still working on the Cloner?' I asked.

His face turned grim and he furtively looked over at the window. 'Sh . . . Not so loud. Someone might hear. I've almost perfected it. I'm nearly there. And this time it is going to pay off.' He led me across the room to a machine that looked something like a telephone box with a whole lot of wires hanging out of it. Down one side were a number of dials and switches. There were two red buttons. One was labelled COPY and the other REVERSE.

Dr Woolley placed a pinecone on the floor of the Cloner. Then he pressed the button that said COPY. There was a whirring sound and a puff of smoke and then, amazingly, the outline of another pinecone, exactly the same as the first, appeared. It lasted for about ten seconds and then the machine started to rock and shake and the whirring slowly died. The image of the second pinecone faded away.

'Fantastic,' I yelled.

'Blast,' said Dr Woolley. 'It's unstable. It won't hold the copy. But I'm nearly there. I think I know how to fix it.'

'What will you use it for?' I asked. 'What's the good of copying pinecones? There are plenty of pinecones already. We don't need more of those.'

He started to get excited. 'Listen, Robert.'

'Tim,' I said.

'Tim, then. It doesn't only work with pinecones. It will work with anything.' He looked up at the window as he said it. Then he dropped his voice. 'What if I made a copy

63

of a bar of gold, eh? What then? And then another copy and another and another. We would be rich. Rich.'

I started to get excited too. I liked the way he said 'we'.

Doctor Woolley started nodding his little head up and down. 'All I need is time,' he said. 'Time to get the adjustment right. Then we will show them whether I'm a crank or not.'

We had a cup of tea together and then I headed off home. That was two good things that had happened in one day. First, Fiona saying she would go with me and second, the Cloner was nearly working. I whistled all the way home.

I didn't see Dr Woolley for some time after that. I had a lot on my mind. I had to walk home with Fiona and every night I went to her place to study with her. Not that we got much study done. On weekends we went hiking or hung around listening to records. It was the best time of my life. There was only one blot on the horizon. Mat Hodson. One of his mates had told me he was out to get me. He left a message saying he was going to flatten me for taking his girl.

His girl! Fiona couldn't stand him. She told me she thought he was a show off and a bully. But that wasn't going to help me. If he wanted to flatten me he would get me in the end. Fortunately he had caught the mumps and had to stay at home for three weeks. Someone had told me it was very painful.

I decided to go round to see Dr Woolley about a month later. I wondered if he had perfected his Cloner. When I reached the door I gave the secret knock but there was no answer. 'That's strange,' I said to myself. 'He never goes out for anything.'

I looked through the window and although the curtains were drawn I could see the light was on inside. I knocked again on the door but still no answer. Then I started to worry. What if he had had a heart attack or something? He could be lying unconscious on the floor. I ran around to the back, got the key from the hiding spot in an old kettle and let myself into the workshop. The place was in a mess. Tables and chairs were turned over and crockery was lying smashed on the floor. It looked as if there had been a fight in the workshop. There was no sign of Dr Woolley.

I started to clean the place up, turning the chairs up the right way and putting the broken things into the bin. That's when I found the letter. It was in an envelope marked with four names. It said, 'John', 'Peter', 'Robert', and 'Tim'. The first three names were crossed out. Dr Woolley had finally remembered my name was Tim after four tries. Inside the letter said:

TIM

IF YOU FIND THIS LETTER SOMETHING TERRIBLE HAS HAPPENED. YOU MUST DESTROY THE CLONER AT ONCE.

WOOLLEY

My eye caught something else on the floor. I went over and picked it up. It was another letter exactly the same as the first. Exactly the same. It even had the three wrong names crossed out. Dr Woolley really was the most absent-minded person.

I looked at the Cloner with a feeling of dread. What

65

had happened? Why did he want me to destroy it? And where was Dr Woolley? The Cloner was switched on. I could tell that because the red light next to REVERSE was shining. I walked over to it and switched it over to COPY. I don't know what made me do it. I guess I just wanted to know if the Cloner worked. I should have left it alone but I didn't. I took a Biro out of my top pocket and threw it inside the Cloner.

Immediately an image of another Biro formed. There were two of them where before there had only been one. I turned the Cloner off and picked up both pens. As far as I could tell they were identical. I couldn't tell which was the real one. They were both real.

I sat down on a chair feeling a bit dizzy. This was the most fantastic machine that had ever been invented. It could make me rich. Dr Woolley had said that it could even copy gold bars. All sorts of wonderful ideas came into my mind. I decided that nothing would make me destroy the Cloner.

I went over and switched the machine on to REVERSE. Then I threw both of the pens into the Cloner. I was shocked by what happened. Both of them disappeared. They were gone. For good. I turned it back to COPY but nothing happened. I tried REVERSE again but still nothing. It was then that I noticed a huge blowfly buzzing around the room. It flew crazily around my head and then headed straight into the Cloner. It vanished without a trace.

The Cloner was dangerous when it was switched on to REVERSE. It could make things vanish for good. I wondered if Dr Woolley had fallen into the machine. Or

66

had he been pushed? There were certainly signs of a struggle.

I thought about going to the Police. But what could they do? They couldn't help Dr Woolley if he had fallen into the Cloner. And they would take it away and I would never see it again. I didn't want that to happen. I had plans for that machine. It was mine now. I was the rightful owner. After all, Dr Woolley had said that 'we' would be rich. Unfortunately now it was just going to be me who was rich.

I went back to Fiona's house and spent the evening doing homework with her. I didn't tell her about the Cloner. I was going to give her the first copies I made from it. At ten o'clock I walked home through the darkened streets, keeping an eye out for Mat Hodson. I had heard he was over his mumps and was looking for me.

The next morning I borrowed Mum's gold cameo brooch without telling her. I decided not to go to school but instead I went to Dr Woolley's workshop. Once inside I turned the Cloner on to COPY and threw in the brooch. Immediately another one appeared. I turned the Cloner off and took out both brooches. One was a mirror image of the other. They both had the same gold setting and the same ivory face. But on one brooch the face looked to the left and on the other it looked to the right. Apart from that they were identical.

I whistled to myself. The copy was so good I couldn't remember which way Mum's brooch had faced. Still it didn't matter. I would put one of them back where I had got it and give the other to Fiona.

67

Next I decided to experiment with something that was alive. I went outside and hunted around in the long grass. After a while I found a small green frog with a black patch on its left side. I took it in and threw it straight into the Cloner. In a flash there were two frogs. They jumped out onto the workshop floor. I picked them up and looked at them. They were both alive and perfectly happy. They were both green but one had a black patch on the left and the other had it on the right. One was a mirror image of the other.

This Cloner was wonderful. I spent all day there making copies of everything I could think of. By four o'clock there was two of almost everything in the workshop. I decided it was time to go and give Fiona her cameo. She was going to be very happy to get it.

I never made it to Fiona's house. An unpleasant surprise was waiting outside for me. It was Mat Hodson.

'I've been waiting for you, you little fink,' he said. 'I heard you were hiding in here.' He had a pair of footy boots hanging around his neck. He was on his way to practice. He gave a nasty leer. 'I thought I told you to stay away from my girl.'

'She's not your girl,' I said hotly. 'She can't stand you. She's my . . .' I never finished the sentence. He hit me with a tremendous punch in the guts and I went down like an exploding balloon. The pain was terrible and I couldn't breathe. I fought for air but nothing happened. I was winded. And all I could do was lay there on the footpath wriggling like a dying worm.

'You get one of those every day,' he said. 'Until you

68

break it off with Fiona.' Then he laughed and went off to footy practice.

After a while my breath started to come back in great sobs and spasms. I staggered back into the workshop and sat down. I was mad. I was out of my mind. I had to think of some way to stop him. I couldn't go through this every day and I couldn't give up Fiona. I needed help. And badly. But I couldn't think of anyone. I didn't have a friend who would help me fight Hodson except Fiona and I couldn't ask her.

My mind was in a whirl and my stomach ached like crazy. I wasn't thinking straight. That's why I did the stupidest thing of my life. I decided to get inside the Cloner and turn it on. There would be two of me. Two Tims. I could get The Copy to help me fight Hodson. He would help me. After all, he would be the same as me. He would want to pay Hodson back as much as I did. The more I thought about it, the smarter it seemed.

I would make an exact copy of myself and together we could go off and flatten Hodson. I wondered what my first words to the new arrival should be. In the end I decided to say, 'Hello there, welcome to earth.' I know it sounds corny but at the time it was all I could think of.

I turned the Cloner to COPY and jumped in before I lost my nerve. In a twinkling there was another 'me' standing there. It was just like looking into a mirror. He had the same jeans, the same jumper and the same brown eyes. We both stood staring at each other for about thirty seconds without saying a thing. Then, both at the same time we said, 'Hello, there, welcome to earth.'

69

That gave me a heck of a shock. How did he know what I was going to say? I couldn't figure it out. It wasn't until much later I realised he knew all about me. He had an exact copy of my brain. He knew everything I had ever done. He knew what I had been thinking before I stepped into the Cloner. That's why he was able to say the same sentence. He knew everything about me. He even knew how many times I had kissed Fiona. The Copy wasn't just a copy. He was me.

We both stood there again for about thirty seconds with our brains ticking over. We were both trying to make sense of the situation. I drew a breath to say something but he beat me to it. 'Well,' he said. 'What are we waiting for? Let's go get Hodson.'

The Copy and I jogged along the street towards the football ground without speaking. I wondered what he was thinking. He didn't know what I was thinking. We shared the same past but not the same future or present. From now on everything that happened would be experienced differently by both of us. I didn't have the faintest idea what was going on in his head. But I knew what was going on in mine. I was wondering how I was going to get rid of him when this was all over.

'Fiona will like that brooch,' said The Copy. I was shocked to think he knew about it. He was smiling to himself. I went red. He was probably thinking Fiona was going to give him a nice big kiss when she saw that brooch. It was me she was going to kiss, not The Copy.

At last we reached the football ground. Hodson was just coming out of the changing rooms. 'Well look,' he said. 'It's little Tim and his twin brother. Brought him to help you, have you?' he said to The Copy. 'Well, I can handle both of you.' He screwed up his hand into a tight fist. Suddenly he looked very big. In fact he looked big enough to wipe the floor with both of us.

I felt like running for it. So did The Copy. I could see he was just about to turn around and run off, leaving me on my own. We both turned and fled. Hodson chased after us for a bit and finally gave it away. 'See you tomorrow, boys,' he yelled. I could hear the other footballers laughing at us. It was humiliating. I knew the others would tell Fiona about what a coward I was.

I turned to The Copy. 'A fat lot of use you turned out to be,' I said.

'What are you talking about,' he replied. 'You're the one who turned and ran off first. You knew I couldn't handle him on my own.'

I realised The Copy was a liar. I decided to go home for tea. He walked along beside me. 'Where do you think you're going?' I asked.

'Home for tea.'

'We can't both turn up for tea. What's Mum going to say when she sees two of us? The shock will kill her,' I told him.

We both kept on walking towards home. The Copy knew the way. He knew everything I knew. Except what I was thinking. He only knew about what had happened before he came out of the Cloner. He didn't know what was going on in my mind after that. I stopped. He seemed determined to come home with me. 'Look,' I said. 'Be reasonable. Think of Mum and Dad. We can't both sit down for tea. You go somewhere else.'

'No,' he said. 'You go somewhere else.'

Finally we came to the front gate. 'All right,' I said to The Copy. 'You go and hide in the bedroom. I'll go down to tea and afterwards I'll sneak you up some food.'

The Copy didn't like it. 'I've got a better idea,' he told me. 'You hide in the bedroom and I'll bring you up something.'

I could see he was only thinking of himself. This thing was turning into a nightmare. 'All right,' I said in the end. 'You go down to tea and I'll hide in the bedroom.' So that is what we did. I sneaked up and hid in my room while The Copy had tea with my parents. It was roast pork. My favourite. I could smell it from my room and it smelt delicious.

The sound of laughter and chattering floated up the stairs. No one knew The Copy wasn't me. They couldn't tell the difference. A bit later he came up the stairs. He poked his head around the corner and threw me a couple of dry biscuits. 'This is all I could find. I'll try and bring you up something later.'

Dry biscuits. I had to eat dry biscuits while The Copy finished off my tea. And I just remembered Mum had been cooking apple pie before we left. This was too much. Something had to be done.

Just then the doorbell rang. 'I'll get it,' shouted The Copy before I had chance to open my mouth. He ran down the stairs and answered the door. I was trapped. I couldn't go down or Mum and Dad would see there were two of us.

I could hear a girl's voice. It was Fiona. A bit later the door closed and all was silent. The Copy had gone outside with her. I raced over to the window and looked out. It was dark but I could just see them under the wattle tree. The street light illuminated the scene. What I saw made my blood boil. The Copy was kissing Fiona. He was kissing my girlfriend. She thought he was me. She couldn't tell the difference and she was letting the creep kiss her. And what is worse she seemed to be enjoying it. It was a very long kiss.

I sat down and thought about the situation. The Copy had to be sent back to where he came from. This whole thing had turned out to be a terrible mistake. I had to get The Copy back to the workshop and get rid of him.

After about two hours The Copy came up to the bedroom looking very pleased with himself. I bit my tongue and didn't say anything about him kissing Fiona. 'Look,' I said. 'We can't both stay here. Why don't we go back to the workshop and have a good talk. Then we can figure out what to do.'

He thought about it for a bit and then he said. 'Okay, you're right. We had better work something out.'

I snuck out of the window and met him outside. We walked all the way to the workshop in silence. I could tell he didn't like me any more than I liked him.

I took the key out of the kettle and let us in. I noticed the Cloner was still switched on to COPY. I went over and turned it on to REVERSE without saying anything. It would all be over quickly. He wouldn't know what hit him. I would just push him straight into the Cloner and everything would be back to normal. He would be gone and there would be just me. It wouldn't be murder. I mean he had only been alive for a few hours and he wasn't really a person. He was just a copy.

'Look,' I said, pointing to the floor of the Cloner. 'Look at this,' I got ready to push him straight in when he came over.

The Copy came over for a look. Suddenly he grabbed me and started to push me towards the machine. The Copy was trying to kill me. He was trying to push me into the Cloner and have Fiona for himself. We fell to the floor in a struggling heap. It was a terrible fight. We both had exactly the same strength and the same experience. As we fought I realised what had happened to Dr Woolley. He had made a copy of himself and they had both tried to push each other in. That's why there were two letters. Probably they had both fallen in and killed each other.

The Copy and I fought for about ten minutes. Neither of us could get the upper hand and we were both growing tired. We rolled over near the bench and I noticed an iron bar on the floor. But The Copy had noticed it too. We both tried to reach it at the same time. But I won. I grabbed it and wrenched my arm free. With a great whack I crashed it down over The Copy's head. He fell to the floor in a heap.

I dragged his lifeless body over to the Cloner and shoved him inside. He vanished without a trace. It was just as if he had never existed. A feeling of great relief spread over me but I was shaking at the narrow escape I had experience. I turned and ran home without even locking up the workshop.

By the time I got home I felt a lot better. I walked into the lounge where Mum and Dad were sitting watching TV. Dad looked up at me. 'Ah there you are, Tim. Would you fill out this application for the school camp? You put in the details and I'll sign the bottom.'

I took the form and started to fill it in. I was looking forward to the school camp. We were going skiing. After a while I looked up. Mum and Dad were both staring at me in a funny way.

'What's up?' I asked.

'You're writing with your left hand,' said Dad.

'So?'

'You've been a right hander all your life.'

'And your hair is parted on the wrong side,' said Mum. And that little mole that used to be on your right cheek has moved to the left side.'

My head started to swim. I ran over to the mirror on the wall. The face that stared back at me was not Tim's. It was the face of The Copy.

STUFFED

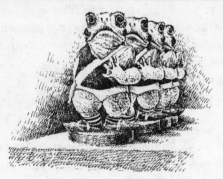

I'll tell you one thing for sure. Fruitcake and Pancake were the best pets that Martin had ever had. Boy, he could train them to do just about anything.

Their best trick was to act as an alarm clock. Martin had rigged up the empty fish tank in his bedroom so that Fruitcake was on one side behind a piece of glass and Pancake was on the other. At exactly seven o'clock a little glass door would swing open and Fruitcake could hop through and stand on Pancake's back. By doing this he could reach up and catch a dead fly with his tongue. The fly hung on a piece of cotton which stretched across the bedroom and was tied to Martin's little toe. When Fruit-cake grabbed the fly with his tongue the cotton would yank on Martin's toe and wake him up.

Martin sure was a brain.

And Fruitcake and Pancake were the smartest cane toads in the whole of Queensland. Martin had even taught them to row a little boat up and down the bath.

76

They were fantastic and Martin loved them just as if they were his children.

Now this might seem a bit strange to you or me because most people think cane toads are just ugly pests that look like frogs and live in the garden. But not Martin. He thought they were beautiful. I have even seen him kiss the two toads full on the mouth.

Don't laugh, because when I tell you how Martin saved the lives of those toads you will understand why he felt this way about them.

You see, there was this bloke call Frisbee who owned a shop near Martin. Frisbee was a great big bloke with a huge beer pot. His stomach hung out so much that his belt had to loop down underneath it. His shop was just out of town in the bush, near where Martin lived.

It was a tourist shop. It sold stuff like real plastic boomerangs and animals made out of shells from the Barrier Reef. He had genuine Aboriginal tapping sticks with elephants carved on them. He also sold a lot of wooden rulers and letter openers made from trees cut down in the rain forests.

His best selling line was his toy koala bears. Once Martin peeked through a chink in the blinds at night and saw Frisbee cutting all the MADE IN JAPAN labels off the koalas. When he had finished he placed little Australian flags in the hands of the koalas.

Every night when he closed up the shop, Frisbee would pull down the blind and put up a stretcher. This was where he slept. He never washed and he never changed his clothes. He lived and slept in the same clothes for years and years.

But all these things are nothing next to what Frisbee used to do to cane toads. He hated cane toads as much as Martin loved them.

Frisbee was a cane toad killer. He used to find a lamp post near a busy road. You know how the insects hang around the street lights and the cane toads hang around too so that they can catch the insects? Well Frisbee used to catch himself a bucket full of cane toads underneath the street lamp. Then he would throw them out onto the road when a car was coming.

Some of the drivers were as mean as Frisbee and they would try to run over the toads. If they missed, Frisbee would yell out 'Fruitcake' at the driver as loud as he could. If the car hit the toad and squashed it flat, Frisbee would yell out 'Pancake' and jump up and down laughing his silly head off.

Sometimes Frisbee and his mean mates would go back a couple of days later. They used to prise the dried-out, flattened toads off the road and throw them to each other like flying saucers. This is how he got the name Frisbee.

Well, on the night I am talking about, Martin was walking down the street right when Frisbee was throwing his last two toads onto the road. Quick as a flash, and without thinking of his own safety, Martin nipped out and grabbed the two toads just as a truck was about to flatten them. Then he nicked off into the bush before Frisbee knew what had happened.

'Come back here, you squirt,' yelled out Frisbee. 'Give those toads back or I'll stuff them down your throat.' He ran off after Martin as fast as he could go. And that was

78

very fast indeed. He was a good runner for a big bloke and he was as mad as a wombat.

Martin was scared as he ran through the dark scrub. He knew he would look like a squashed toad himself if Frisbee got hold of him so he did the only thing he could think of. He charged off into Tiger Snake Swamp which lay at the bottom of the hill.

Now there are only two things which live in Tiger Snake Swamp. There are cane toads and they wouldn't hurt a fly (so to speak), and tiger snakes, which are deadly poisonous. Also, it is possible to get lost in Tiger Snake Swamp because it covers hundreds of square kilometres with twisted trees and murky waterways.

Martin knew that it was dangerous, especially at night. He waded out through the weeds until he was up to his waist.

Frisbee was too chicken to go in the water so he just stood on the bank yelling and swearing at Martin. In the end he said, 'Don't think you are going to get away with this, toad lover. I am going to fix you up. For good. Your little toad-clearing business will soon be wiped out.' Then he turned round and stormed off into the night.

At this stage I should tell you about Martin's toad-clearing business. On weekends Martin used to go around to houses and offer to clear out all of the toads from people's back yards. Martin couldn't figure out why people didn't like to have thirty or so toads in their gardens. He didn't realise that some people were scared of them. Others didn't like standing on them in their bare feet at night. It was a bit yucky scraping the green and yellow stuff out from between their toes.

For three dollars Martin would collect all their toads and then let them go in Tiger Snake Swamp.

What he didn't know was that Frisbee was about to go into the toad business himself. In a big way.

As he waded out of the water Martin noticed that there were hundreds and hundreds of cane toads around him. Some of them looked familiar. Martin was the only person in the world who could remember the faces of toads. Most people think they all look the same. 'G'day, Dodger,' he said to one large toad. 'Aren't you the one I found in Mrs French's outside laundry?'

The toad gave a loud grunt as if to say yes.

Martin made his way home from the swamp with the two toads he had rescued from the road. 'I'll keep you two,' he said. 'I'll call you toads Fruitcake and Pancake. You might bring me luck.'

The two toads did bring Martin luck. Bad luck. As the months went by Martin found that his toad-clearing business went from bad to worse. Every house he went to had already been cleared out. No one wanted toads removed any more and he couldn't work out why.

Then one day he saw an ad. in the local paper. It said:

TOAD STUFFERS PTY LTD
CANE TOADS REMOVED
FREE
PHONE 505 64 0111

No wonder he couldn't get any more toad-clearing jobs. Someone was doing it for nothing.

Martin rang the phone number to see who it was but

80

he already knew who was going to answer the phone. He wasn't wrong. It was Frisbee.

As soon as he heard Frisbee's voice, Martin sadly hung up the phone without saying anything.

That night Martin hid behind a tree and waited outside Frisbee's shop. At seven-thirty Frisbee left the house pulling a large box of wheels. He walked into town and went into the back yard of a flash-looking house. Martin looked over the fence. Frisbee was fishing around behind the plants with a torch looking for cane toads. Every time he caught one, he gave its neck a quick twist and threw the lifeless body into the box.

'Murderer,' gasped Martin under his breath. He wanted to rush over and stop Frisbee from killing the toads but he knew he wasn't strong enough. Frisbee was just too big for him.

When the box was full, Frisbee made his way back to his shop on the edge of town. He took the box inside and shut the door.

Martin peeked in through a crack in the blinds. What he saw made him shudder with horror. Frisbee put a hook thing into a toad's mouth and pulled out all the innards. Then he shoved in some cotton wool in place of the gizzards and painted the toad with a clear liquid. Next he put a little skirt on the toad and placed a small tennis racquet in its hand. He sat it on a wire stand on a shelf next to another stuffed toad which also had a tennis racquet. A little net was stretched between the toads. It looked just as if they were playing tennis.

Frisbee wrote something on a piece of cardboard and placed it next to the stuffed toads. It said:

Frisbee gave a wicked chuckle as he looked at his work. Then he reached into the box and took out another dead toad.

Martin felt sick. The shelves of the hut were lined with stuffed toads. Hundreds and hundreds of them. Some were sitting inside little toy cars. Others held tiny fishing rods. One pair was kissing. There was even a toad sitting on a tiny toilet. And all of them had price tags.

At first Martin didn't know what was going on. Then he realised that Frisbee was killing all the toads he caught and stuffing them. Then he was selling the stuffed toads to tourists from down south. Martin noticed eighteen toads all dressed in little red and white football jumpers. The Sydney Swans. On another shelf the whole Collingwood team of toads was lined up.

This was the cruellest, meanest, most horrible thing that he had ever heard of. Martin knew that he had to stop this fiendish business but he didn't know what to do. He was only a pipsqueak next to Frisbee.

Then he had an idea. He walked home with a spring in his step. He would come back one night when Frisbee wasn't there. He would stop him stuffing toads once and for all.

Two weeks later, Martin crept up to Frisbee's shop. It was late in the night and very dark. Frisbee had gone off catching cane toads. Or that's what Martin thought anyway. He looked around into the blackness but saw nothing. Something rustled in the bushes. He hoped it was a toad or a rat.

Shivers ran down his spine. If something went wrong

82

there was nothing to help him. He took his father's pair of bolt cutters and cut through the padlock on the shop door. Then he went inside and turned on the light. Light filled the room for a second and then vanished. The globe had blown.

Martin switched on his torch and looked around. The stuffed toads looked eerie in the torchlight. 'I hope toads don't have ghosts,' he said to himself. 'Because if they do I'm a goner.' He looked at the tennis toads. They stood there as if frozen in the middle of an imaginary game.

He picked up the tennis toads. They were hard and lifeless. 'I'm going to give you a proper burial,' said Martin. He put them down and reached into a small sack.

In the silent night a twig snapped. He had to hurry. There was a sound of footsteps approaching. Someone was coming. He quickly finished, switched out his torch and slipped out of the door into the blackness.

And there stood Frisbee. Even in the dark Martin could see that his face was twisted up in rage. He let out a bellow and charged at Martin with outstretched hands. Martin turned and fled. He ran and crashed through the undergrowth. Branches scratched his legs and face but he didn't feel them. All he felt were his bursting lungs and the deep fear of what Frisbee would do to him if he caught him. He ran blindly, not even realising that he had come once again to Tiger Snake Swamp. He plunged into the water as before.

But this time Frisbee followed. Martin felt himself grabbed by strong hands and pushed under the water. He couldn't breathe. He tried to struggle free but Frisbee was too strong. Martin held his breath but the seconds seemed like hours. He knew that he would have to open his mouth and breathe in lungfuls of water. His chest hurt.

And then, suddenly, he was released. Frisbee let go.

Martin burst upwards and gulped in air. Then he looked at Frisbee. He saw an unbelievable sight. Frisbee was completely covered in a swarming sea of cane toads. They crawled over his shoulders and face and hair. He looked like a moving green bee hive.

He screamed and yelled. 'Get them off. Get them off.' He scraped at them with both hands but for every one that he threw away another ten clambered on to the pile.

Frisbee struggled to the shore under the seething skin of toads. He grabbed a branch and started scraping them from his body. Then he staggered back towards his shop.

Martin followed at a safe distance. As he went he passed dead and dying toads. He could see that Frisbee was winning the battle and the covering of toads was thinning out. By the time Frisbee reached the shop there was only one toad left. Frisbee plucked it from his hair and threw it on the ground. Then he stamped on it viciously. And went into the shop, slamming the door behind him.

Martin smiled and quickly hooked the broken padlock through the latch.

'You're locked in,' he yelled to Frisbee. 'I'm not letting you out until you promise not to kill any more toads.'

There was a furious rattling as Frisbee shook the door. 'Let me out or I'll skin you alive,' he shouted. 'That's the only promise you'll get out of me.'

'Okay,' said Martin. 'See you later then.'

Frisbee heard footsteps disappear into the night.

Inside the shop it was dark. There was only a little moonlight filtering through the cracks in the blinds. The stuffed toads were silvery. They looked ghostly, sitting all around him on the shelves. Frisbee shivered. Then he went over and shook the door again. It was firmly locked. He could easily get out by smashing the window but he wasn't going to do that. A customer could let him out in the morning.

He set up his stretcher on the floor and sat on it. Then he opened a stubby and started swigging his beer.

The dead toads stared at him silently. The night was still. He heard a small shuffle. 'What was that?' he gasped aloud. There was no answer.

He looked at the toad captain of the Collingwood Football Team. Its eyes seemed to stare back. Frisbee blinked his eyes and looked again. A cold shiver ran up his spine. Had that football toad blinked? Surely not. It couldn't. It was dead.

From the shelves hundreds and hundreds of dead toads peered down at him. Their eyes seemed to say 'murderer'.

'Nonsense,' whispered Frisbee to himself. 'Dead toads don't know anything. Neither do live ones for that matter.' He felt foolish for whispering.

He heard another scuffle in the silence and jumped. He looked at the toad with the fishing rod. Had that line moved? Surely not.

85

For the first time in his life Frisbee was scared. He was terrified. The stuffed toads seemed to stare at him as if any moment they might jump down and attack him. He remembered that the Rambo toad had a sharp little hunting knife in its hand.

He heard another soft movement behind him. He looked around suddenly and nearly fainted with fear. One of the tennis toads was moving. He was sure of it. He could see its throat pulsing as if it was breathing. Suddenly the toad lifted up its tiny tennis racquet and threw its little ball into the air. It hit the ball over the net.

Frisbee rubbed his eyes and screamed out loud. The toad on the other side of the net returned the serve.

The stuffed toads were playing tennis.

Frisbee charged at the locked door. His terror gave him super strength and he burst the door from its hinges and ran screaming into the night.

Martin laughed gently from his hiding place behind a tree. Then he walked into the shed and picked up the two tennis toads. 'Well, Pancake and Fruitcake,' he said. 'It was hard work teaching you to play tennis. But it sure was worth it.'

NO IS YES

The question is: did the girl kill her own father? Some say yes and some say no.

Linda doesn't look like a murderess.

She walks calmly up the steps of the high school stage. She shakes the mayor's hand and receives her award. Top of the school. She moves over to the microphone to make her speech of acceptance. She is seventeen, beautiful and in love. Her words are delicate, musical crystals falling upon receptive ears. The crowd rewards her clarity with loud applause but it passes her by. She is seeking a face among the visitors in the front row. She finds what she is looking for and her eyes meet those of a young man. They both smile.

He knows the answer.

'It's finally finished,' said Dr Scrape. 'After fourteen years of research it is finished.' He tapped the thick manuscript on the table. 'And you, Ralph, will be the first to see the results.'

87

They were sitting in the lounge watching the sun lower itself once more into the grave of another day.

Ralph didn't seem quite sure what to say. He was unsure of himself. In the end he came out with. 'Fourteen years is a lot of work. What's it all about?'

Dr Scrape stroked his pointed little beard and leaned across the coffee table. 'Tell me,' he said, 'As a layman, how did you learn to speak? How did you learn the words and grammar of the English language?'

'Give us a go,' said Ralph good naturedly. 'I haven't had an education like you. I haven't been to university. I didn't even finish high school. I don't know about stuff like that. You're the one with all the brains. You tell me. How did I learn to speak?'

When Ralph said, 'You're the one with all the brains,' Dr Scrape smiled to himself and nodded wisely. 'Have a guess then,' he insisted.

'Me mother. Me mother taught me to talk.'

'No.'

'Me father then.'

'No.'

'Then who?' asked Ralph with a tinge of annoyance.

'Nobody taught you,' exclaimed Dr Scrape. 'Nobody teaches children to talk. They just learn it by listening. If the baby is in China it will learn Chinese because that's what it hears. If you get a new-born Chinese baby and bring it here it will learn to speak English not Chinese. Just by listening to those around it.'

'What's that got to do with your re . . .?' began Ralph. But he stopped. Dr Scrape's daughter entered the room

88

with a tray. She was a delicate, pale girl of about four-teen. Her face reminded Ralph of a porcelain doll. He was struck by both her beauty and her shyness.

'This is my daughter, Linda,' said Dr Scrape with a flourish.

'G'day,' said Ralph awkwardly.

'And this is Mr Pickering.'

She made no reply at first but simply stood there staring at him as if he were a creature from another planet. He felt like some exotic animal in the zoo which was of total fascination to someone on the other side of the bars.

Dr Scrape frowned and the girl suddenly remembered her manners.

'How do you do?' she said awkwardly. 'Would you like some coffee?'

'Thanks a lot,' said Ralph.

'White or black?'

'Black, thanks.'

Linda raised an eyebrow at her father. 'The usual for me,' he said with a smirk. Ralph Pickering watched as Linda poured two cups of tea and put milk into both of them. She looked up, smiled and handed him one of the cups.

'Thanks a lot,' he said again.

'Salt?' she asked, proferring a bowl filled with white crystals.

Ralph looked at the bowl with a red face. He felt uncomfortable in this elegant house. He didn't know the right way to act. He didn't have the right manners. He didn't know why he had been asked in for a cup of coffee.

He was just the apprentice plumber here to fix the drains. He looked down at his grubby overalls and mud encrusted shoes.

'Er, eh?' said Ralph.

'Salt?' she asked again holding out the bowl.

Ralph shook his head with embarrassment. Did they really have salt in their tea? He sipped from the delicate china cup. He liked coffee, black and with sugar, in a nice big mug. Somehow he had ended up with white tea, no sugar and a fragile cup which rattled in his big hands.

He had the feeling, though, that Linda had not meant to embarrass him. If there was any malevolence it came from Dr Scrape who was grinning hugely at Ralph's discomfort.

Ralph Pickering scratched his head with his broken fingernails.

The young girl looked at her watch. 'Will you be staying for breakfast?' she asked Ralph kindly. 'We are having roast pork. It's nearly washed.'

'N, n, no thanks,' he stumbled. 'My mum is expecting me home for tea. I couldn't stay the night.' He noticed a puzzled expression on her face and she shook her head as if not quite understanding him. The oddest feeling came over him that she thought he was a bit mad.

Ralph moved as if to stand up.

'Don't go yet,' said Dr Scrape. 'I haven't finished telling you about my research. Although you have already seen some of it.' He nodded towards his daughter who had gone into the kitchen and could be heard preparing the pork for the evening meal. 'Now where were we?' he went on. 'Ah yes. About learning to speak. So you see, my dear boy, we learn to speak just

90

from hearing those around us talking.' He was waving his hands around as if delivering a lecture to a large audience. His eyes lit up with excitement. 'But ask yourself this. What if a child was born and never heard anyone speak except on the television? Never ever saw a real human being, only the television? Would the television do just as well as live people? Could they learn to talk then?'

He paused, not really expecting Ralph to say anything. Then he answered his own question. 'No one knows,' he exclaimed thrusting a finger into the air. 'It's never been done.'

'It would be cruel,' said Ralph, suddenly forgetting his shyness. 'You couldn't bring up a child who had never heard anyone speak. It'd be a dirty trick. That's why it's never been done.'

'Right,' yelled Dr Scrape. His little beard was waggling away as he spoke. 'So I did the next best thing. I never let her hear anybody speak except me.' He nodded towards the kitchen.

'You mean . . .' began Ralph.

'Yes, yes. Linda. My daughter. She has never heard anyone in the world speak except me. You are the first person apart from me she has ever spoken to.'

'You mean she has never been to school?'

'No.'

'Or kindergarten?'

'No.'

'Or shopping or to the beach?'

'No, she's never been out of this house.'

'But why?' asked Ralph angrily. 'What for?'

'It's an experiment, boy. She has learned a lot of

91

words incorrectly. Just by listening to me use the wrong words. All without a single lesson. I call "up" "down" and "down" "up". I call "sugar" "salt". "Yes" is "no" and "no" is "yes". It's been going on ever since she was a baby. I have taught her thousands of words incorrectly. She thinks that room in there is called the laundry,' he yelled pointing to the kitchen. 'I have let her watch television every day and all day but it makes no difference. She can't get it right.'

He picked up a spoon and chuckled. 'She calls this a carpet. And this,' he said holding up a fork, 'she calls a chicken. Even when she sees a chicken on television she doesn't wake up. She doesn't change. She doesn't notice it. It proves my hypothesis: point that is,' he added for the benefit of Ralph whom he considered to be an idiot. 'So you see, I have made a big breakthrough. I have proved that humans can't learn to speak properly from listening to television. Real people are needed.'

'You know something,' said Ralph slowly. 'If this is true, if you have really taught the poor kid all the wrong words . . .'

Dr Scrape interrupted. 'Of course it's true. Of course it's true.' He took out a worn exercise book and flipped over the pages. 'Here they are. Over two thousand words – all learned incorrectly. Usually the opposites. Whenever I talk with Linda I use these words. She doesn't know the difference. Dog is cat, tree is lamp post, ant is elephant and just for fun girl is boy – she calls herself a boy although of course she knows she is the opposite sex to you. She would call you a girl.' He gave a low, devilish laugh.

92

Ralph's anger had completely swamped his shyness and his feeling of awkwardness caused by the splendour of the mansion. 'You are a dirty mongrel,' he said quietly. 'The poor thing has never met another person but you – and what a low specimen you are. And you've mixed her all up. How is she going to get on in the real world?'

'You mean in on the real world, not on in the real world,' he smirked. Then he began to laugh. He thought it was a great joke. 'You'll have to get used to it,' he said. 'When you talk to her you'll have to get used to everything being back to front.'

'What's it got to do with me?'

'Why, I want you to try her out. Talk to her. See how she goes. Before I give my paper and show her to the world I want to make sure that it lasts. That she won't break down and start speaking correctly with strangers. I want you to be the first test. I want a common working man . . . boy,' he corrected. 'One who can't pull any linguistic tricks.'

'Leave me out of it,' said Ralph forcefully. 'I don't want any part of it. It's cruel and, and,' he searched around for a word. 'Rotten,' he spat out.

Scrape grabbed his arm and spun him round. He was dribbling with false sincerity. 'But if you really care, if you really care about her you will try to help. Go on,' he said pushing Ralph towards the kitchen. 'Tell her what a despicable creature I am. Tell her the difference between salt and sugar. Set her straight. That's the least you can do. Or don't you care at all?' he narrowed his eyes.

Ralph pushed him off and strode towards the kitchen.

93

Then he stopped and addressed Scrape who had been following enthusiastically. 'You don't come then. I talk to her alone. Just me and her.'

The little man stroked his beard thoughtfully. 'A good idea,' he said finally. 'A good idea. They will want an independent trial. They might think I am signalling her. A good thought, boy. But I will be close by. I will be in here, in the library. She calls it the toilet,' he added gleefully. Then he burst into a sleazy cackle.

Ralph gave him a look of disgust and then turned and pushed into the kitchen.

Linda turned round from where she was washing the dishes and took several steps backwards. Her face was even paler than before. Ralph understood now that she was frightened of him. Finally, however, she summoned up her courage and stepped forward, holding out her hand. 'Goodbye,' she said in a shaking voice.

'Goodbye?' queried Ralph. 'You want me to go?'

'Yes,' she said, shaking her head as she spoke.

Ralph took her outstretched hand and shook it. It was not a hand shake that said goodbye. It was warm and welcoming.

'Is this really the first time you have been alone with another person other than him?' asked Ralph, nodding towards the library.

'Don't call him a person,' she said with a hint of annoyance. 'We don't let persons in the laundry. Only animals are allowed here. The cats have kennels in the river.'

'You've got everything back to front,' said Ralph incredulously. 'All your words are mixed up.'

'Front to back,' she corrected, staring at him with a

puzzled face. 'And you are the one with everything mixed down. You talk strangely. Are you drunk? I have heard that women behave strangely when they are drunk.'

Ralph's head began to spin. He couldn't take it all in. He didn't trust himself to speak. He remembered Dr Scrape's words, 'Dog is cat, tree is lamp post, ant is elephant, and just for fun, boy is girl.' Linda was looking at him as if he was mad. He walked over to the sink and picked up a fork. 'What's this?' he said, waving it around excitedly.

'A chicken of course,' she answered. Ralph could see by her look that she thought he was the one with the crazy speech.

'And what lays eggs and goes cluck, cluck?' He flapped his arms like wings as he said it.

The girl smiled with amusement. 'A fork. Haven't you ever seen a fork scratching for bananas?'

Ralph hung his head in his hands. 'Oh no,' he groaned. 'The swine has really mucked you up. You have got everything back to front – front to back. They don't dig for bananas. They dig for worms.' He stared at her with pity-filled eyes. She was completely confused. She was also the most beautiful girl he had ever seen. He bit his knuckles and thought over the situation carefully. 'Man' was 'woman'. 'Boy' was 'girl'. 'Ceiling' was 'floor'. But some words were right. 'Him' and 'her' were both correct. Suddenly he turned and ran from the room. He returned a second later holding Dr Scrape's exercise book. He flicked wildly through the pages, groaning and shaking his head as he read.

The girl looked frightened. She held her head up like a

95

deer sniffing the wind. 'That glass must not be read,' she whispered, looking nervously towards the library. 'None of the glasses in the toilet can be read either.'

He ignored her fear. 'Now,' he said to himself. 'Let's try again.' He held the exercise book open in one hand for reference. Then he said slowly, 'Have you ever spoken to a girl like me before?'

'Yes,' said Linda shaking her head.

Ralph sighed and then tried again. He held up the fork. 'Is this a chicken?'

'No,' she said nodding her head. Ralph could see that she was regarding him with a mixture of fear, amusement and, yes, he would say, affection. Despite her bewilderment over what she considered to be his strange speech, she liked him.

Suddenly the enormity of the crime that had been worked on this girl overwhelmed Ralph. He was filled with anger and pity. And disgust with Dr Scrape. Linda had never been to school. Never spoken to another person. Never been to the movies or a disco. For fourteen years she had spoken only to that monster Scrape. She had been a prisoner in this house. She had never been touched by another person ... never been kissed.

Their eyes met for an instant but the exchange was put to flight by the sound of coughing coming from the library.

'Quick,' said Ralph. 'There isn't much time. I want you to nod for "yes" and shake your head for "no" – drat, I mean the other way around.' He consulted the exercise book. 'I mean nod your head for "no" and shake your head for "yes". He looked again at the book. The words

96

were alphabetically listed. He couldn't be sure that she understood. What if the word for head was foot? Or the word for shake was dance, or something worse?

Linda paused and then nodded.

He tried again. 'Have you ever spoken to another animal except him?' he said jerking a contemptuous thumb in the direction of the library.

She shook her head sadly. It was true then. Scrape's story was true.

'Would you like to?' he asked slowly after finding that 'like' was not listed in the book.

She paused, looked a little fearful, and then keeping her eyes on his, nodded her head slowly.

'Tonight,' he whispered, and then, checking the book, 'No, today. At midnight, no sorry, midday. I will meet you. By that lamp post.' He pointed out of the window and across the rolling lawns of the mansion. 'By that lamp post. Do you understand?'

Linda followed his gaze. There was a lamp post at the far end of the driveway which could just be seen through the leaves of a large gum tree in the middle of the lawn. He took her hand. It was warm and soft and sent a current of happiness up his arm. He asked her again in a whisper. 'Do you understand?'

She nodded and for the first time he noticed a sparkle in her eyes.

'I didn't ask you to maul my son,' a voice hissed from behind them. Ralph jumped as a grip of steel took hold of his arm. Dr Scrape was incredibly strong. He dragged Ralph out of the kitchen and into the lounge. 'You stay in the laundry,' he snarled at Linda as the kitchen door swung closed in her face.

97

'Well, my boy,' he said with a twisted grin. 'How did it go? Could you make head or tail of what she said? Or should I say tail or head?' He licked his greasy moustache with satisfaction at his little joke.

Ralph tried to disguise the contempt he felt. 'What would happen if she mixed with people in the real world?' he asked. 'If she was to leave here and go to school? Would she learn to talk normally?'

Dr Scrape paused and looked carefully at Ralph as if reading his mind. 'Yes,' he said. 'Of course she would. She would model on the others. She would soon speak just like you I suspect. But that's not going to happen, is it?'

Ralph could contain himself no longer. 'You devil,' he yelled. 'You've mucked her up all right. She thinks I am the one who can't talk properly. She thinks I'm a bit crazy. But don't think I'm going to help you. I'll do everything I can to stop you. You're nothing but a vicious, crazy little monster.' He stood up and stormed out of the house.

Dr Scrape gave a wicked smile of satisfaction as Ralph disappeared down the long driveway.

It was thirty minutes past midnight and a few stars appeared occasionally when the drifting clouds allowed them to penetrate.

It was a different Ralph who stood waiting beneath the lamp post. Gone were the overalls, work boots and the smudged face. He wore his best jeans and his hair shone in the light of the street light. He had taken a lot of time over his appearance.

He looked anxiously at his watch and then up at the

dark house. There was no sign of Linda. She was thirty minutes late. His heart sank as slowly and surely as the sun had done that evening. She wasn't coming. She had dismissed him as a funny-speaking crank. Or that evil man had guessed their plan and locked her in a room.

It began to drizzle and soon trickles of water ran down his neck. One o'clock and still no sign of her. He sighed and decided to go. There was nothing more he could do. She wasn't going to show up. The words started to keep time with his feet as he crunched homewards along the gravel road. 'Show up, show up.' Linda would have said 'show down' not 'show up.'

A bell rang in the back of his mind. A tiny, insistent bell of alarm. Once again he heard Dr Scrape speaking. 'Dog is cat, tree is lamp post, ant is . . .' Of course.

'Tree is lamp post. And therefore . . . lamp post is tree.' He almost shouted the words out. She called a lamp post a tree. Linda might have been waiting beneath the gum tree in the middle of the gardens while he was waiting under the lamp post by the gate. He hardly dared hope. He ran blindly in the dark night. Several times he fell over. Once he put a hole in the knee of his jeans but he didn't give it a thought.

He knew that she would have gone. Like him she would have given up waiting and have returned to the dark house.

At last he stumbled up to the tree, finding it by its silhouette against the black sky. 'Linda,' he whispered urgently, using her name for the first time. It tasted sweet on his lips.

There was no answer.

99

Then, at the foot of the house, in the distance, he saw a flicker of yellow light. It looked like a candle. He saw Linda, faintly, holding the small flame. Before he could call out she opened the front door and disappeared inside.

'Damn and blast,' he said aloud. He smashed his clenched fist into the trunk of the tree in disappointment. A lump of bitter anguish welled up in his throat. He threw himself heavily down on the damp ground to wait. Perhaps she would try again. Anyway, he resolved to stay there until morning.

Inside the dark house Linda made her way back to her bedroom upstairs. Her eyes were wet with tears of rejection. The strange girl had not come. She crept silently, terrified of awaking her tormentor. Holding the forbidden candle in her left hand she tiptoed up the stairs. She held her breath as she reached the landing lest her guardian should feel its gentle breeze even from behind closed doors.

'Betrayed, betrayed,' shrieked a figure from the darkness. The candle was struck from her hand and spiralled over the handrail to the floor below. It spluttered dimly in the depths.

The dark form of Dr Scrape began slapping Linda's frail cheeks. Over and over he slapped, accompanying every blow with same shrill word. 'Betrayed, betrayed, betrayed.'

In fear, in shock, in desperation, the girl pushed at the flaying shadow. Losing his footing, Scrape tumbled backwards, over and over, down the wooden staircase. He came to a halt halfway down and lay still.

Linda collapsed onto the top step, sobbing into her

100

hands, not noticing the smoke swirling up from below. Then, awakened to her peril by the crackling flames that raced up the stairs, she filled her lungs with smoke-filled air, screamed and fainted dead away.

The old mansion was soon burning like a house of straws. Flames leapt from the windows and leaked from the tiles. Smoke danced before the moonless sky.

The roar of falling timber awakened Ralph from a fitful doze at the base of the tree. He ran, blindly, wildly, unthinkingly through the blazing front door and through the swirling smoke, made out Linda's crumpled form at the top of the staircase. He ran to her, jumping three steps at a time, ignoring the scorching flames and not feeling the licking pain on his legs. Staggering, grunting, breathing smoke he struggled with her limp body past the unconscious form of Dr Scrape. He paused, and saw in that second that Scrape was still breathing and that his eyes were wide and staring. He seemed unable to move. Ralph charged past him, forward, through the burning door and along the winding driveway. Only the sight of an ambulance and fire truck allowed him to let go and fall with his precious load, unconscious on the wet grass.

'Smoke inhalation,' yelled the ambulance driver. 'Get oxygen and put them both in the back.'

Linda's eyes flickered open and she stared in awe from the stretcher at the uniformed figure. Only the third person she had seen in her life. A mask was lowered over her face, but not before she had time to notice that the unconscious Ralph was breathing quietly on the stretcher next to her.

'I want to speak to her,' yelled the fire chief striding

over from the flashing truck.

'No way, they are both going to hospital,' shouted the ambulance driver in answer.

The fire chief ignored the reply and tore the mask from Linda's gasping mouth. He bent close to her. 'I can't send men in there,' he yelled, pointing at the blazing house. 'Not unless there is someone inside. Is there anyone inside?'

'Mother,' whispered the girl.

The fireman looked around. 'She said mother.'

'She hasn't got a mother,' said a short bald man who had come over from the house next door. 'Her mother died when the girl was born. She only has a father. Dr Scrape.'

The fireman leaned closer. His words were urgent. 'Is your father in there, girl? Is anyone in there? The roof is about to collapse. Is anyone inside the house?'

Linda tried to make sense of his strange speech. Then a look of enlightenment swept across her face. She understood the question – that was clear. But many have wondered if she understood her own answer.

As the ambulance driver shut the door she just had time to say one word.

'No.'

A Little Bit
From the Author
Part 3

Probably you shouldn't read this unless you have a special interest in horse manure or my early life as a boy.

I was six when I came to Australia. By the time I was nine I had a proper Australian accent and now nobody will believe that I was born in England.

We lived in Moorabbin in Victoria. The roads weren't made and there were paddocks all around the house. My father was an engineer but he couldn't get a job. Eventually someone offered him work on an ice-cart. Only rich people had fridges when I was a boy. The rest of us had ice-chests. Dad wouldn't take the job. He said it had no future because everyone would have a fridge one day. We thought he was crazy.

Once a week the ice man would bring around a huge block of ice and put it in the chest. He would deliver the ice on a horse and cart. Often the horse would – well you know – drop a load of manure in the road. My mother would say, 'Quick, Paul, run out and get those horse droppings for the vegetable garden.'

I would screw up my face. 'No way,' I would say, 'What if someone sees me?'

'Hurry up,' she would answer. 'Before the lady over the road gets it.'

I hated getting that horse manure. We had a huge pile of it in the backyard. Talk about embarrassing.

One Christmas Eve my mum said, 'You know those old people who live over the other side of town – the Bunces. They don't have any children so we would like to give them a special Christmas present. You and Ruth can fill up the wheelbarrow with horse manure and take it around to them in the morning.

Oh, the shame of it. 'No way,' I yelled. 'Never. Everyone will see us. On Christmas Day too. We're not going.'

Of course we had to go. When you are a kid you have no power. My sister and I got up at six o'clock so that no one would see us. We filled up the barrow with the stinking droppings. We sneaked out to the front gate. And there were all the kids out on their new bikes. Oh no. They saw us. We started to run with the barrow. Horse manure fell off onto the road. It got on our shoes. It slopped everywhere. The kids all followed us, yelling and laughing and calling out rude things like, 'Look what they got for Christmas.'

Boy, was my face red. I thought we would never get there. But in the end we did. I looked at Ruth. 'This manure is the only thing the Bunces are getting for Christmas,' I said. 'So we'd better make sure that they see it.' We tipped the manure out against their front door and went home.

I could never figure out why the Bunces didn't ring up and say thanks for the present. I guess they didn't like it when they opened the door and the horse manure fell onto their carpet.

Two good things came of all this. One was my father getting a job. He ended up being the works manager of a factory that made fridges. The other good thing happened thirty years later. I wrote a story called 'Cow Dung Custard'* about a poor kid who has to take manure across town in a wheelbarrow.

Paul Jennings

* *'Cow Dung Custard' is published in* Unreal!.

About Paul Jennings

'The biggest sin in writing is to be boring.'
Paul Jennings

Paul Jennings's amazing success story began in December 1985, when *Unreal!* was published in Australia. Within months it was on the best-seller lists and in every child's schoolbag, and there it has stayed. It's been the same story with every book ever since.

Spooky, funny, naughty, yucky, always wacky, and always with a surprise ending, Paul's stories are devoured by readers of all ages. Every year his books top the lists of nominations for the Australian state awards chosen by children. In 1992, Paul won an award in every children's choice list throughout Australia.

In 1990, a thirteen-part television series based upon Paul's early stories was screened in Australia and in the UK. *Round the Twist* received critical acclaim from both countries. The second series, screened in 1993, was the top-rated children's program in both countries. Both series have since been shown in over forty countries throughout the world. Paul wrote the screenplays, and both times he won an AWGIE (Australian Writer's Guild)

Award. The second series was also a finalist for Oustanding Achievement in Programming for Children and Young People in the 1993 International Emmy Awards.

In the United States, *Unmentionable!* was named an ALA Recommended Book for Reluctant Readers; *Unreal!* and *Uncanny!* were both Bank Street College Children's Books of the Year; and *Unreal!* was on New York Public Library's list of "100 Titles for Reading and Sharing".

More than two million copies of Paul Jennings's books have been sold throughout the world. He receives thousands of fan letters every year and replies to them all (if they include a return address).

"Jennings has found the perfect formula for the scary and supernatural sprinkled with just the right touch of hilarity . . . Don't miss out on the fun here."

School Library Journal,
starred review for Unreal!

108

OTHER TERRIFIC BOOKS BY PAUL JENNINGS!
☆☆☆☆☆☆☆☆☆☆☆☆☆☆☆☆☆☆☆☆☆☆☆☆☆☆☆☆☆

Do you loved to be surprised? Grossed out? A little bit scared? Then you'll want to get your hands on these books!

Unreal!
Eight Surprising Stories

These spooky stories will really rattle your bones!

A Bank Street Children's Book of the Year
New York Public Library '100 Titles for Reading and Sharing'
Winner of the 1987 Young Australians' Best Book Award
Winner of the 1989 West Australian Young Readers' Book Award
Winner of the 1990 Kids Own Australian Literature Award
Winner of the 1992 Kids Reading Oz Choice Award

Uncanny!
Even More Surprising Stories

More twists, more laughs, and more scares, and each of these wild stories ends with an uncanny surprise!

A Bank Street Children's Book of the Year
Winner of the 1989 Young Australians' Best Book Award
Winner of the 1992 West Australian Young Readers' Book Award

OTHER TERRIFIC BOOKS BY PAUL JENNINGS!
☆☆☆☆☆☆☆☆☆☆☆☆☆☆☆☆☆☆☆☆☆☆☆☆☆☆☆☆

Unbelievable!
More Surprising Stories

You'll never guess what's going to happen, because these stories are really unbelievable!

Winner of the 1988 Young Australians' Best Book Award
Winner of the 1990 Kids Reading Oz Choice Award

Unbearable!
More Bizarre Stories

More outrageous reading that you won't want to put down!

Winner of the 1993 Young Australians' Best Book Award
Winner of the 1991 and 1993 Kids Own Australian Literature Award

OTHER TERRIFIC BOOKS BY PAUL JENNINGS!
☆☆☆☆☆☆☆☆☆☆☆☆☆☆☆☆☆☆☆☆☆☆☆☆☆☆☆☆

Unmentionable!
More Amazing Stories

Locked in the bathroom ... Kissing a cold, cold kid ... Burning your behind ... it could only be by Paul Jennings!

An ALA Recommended Book for Reluctant Readers
Winner of the 1992 Young Australians' Best Book Award
Winner of the 1992 Kids Own Australian Literature Award

Undone!
More Mad Endings

Plans come undone. Zippers come undone. Bullies come undone. And so will the readers who try to predict the endings of these stories!

Winner of the 1993 Kids Reading Oz Choice Award